SPECIAL EFFECT

RUSSELL J.
SANDERS

Harmony Ink

Published by

Harmony Ink Press
5032 Capital Circle SW
Suite 2, PMB# 279
Tallahassee, FL 32305-7886
USA
publisher@harmonyinkpress.com
http://harmonyinkpress.com

Special Effect
© 2014 Russell J. Sanders.

Cover Art
© 2014 Aaron Anderson.
aaronbydesign55@gmail.com
Cover content is for illustrative purposes only
and any person depicted on the cover is a model.

ISBN: 978-1-62798-911-4
Library ISBN: 978-1-62798-913-8
Digital ISBN: 978-1-62798-912-1

Printed in the United States of America
First Edition
May 2014

Library Edition
August 2014

For my mother, who first took me to the theater, which started a lifelong obsession and devotion.

ACKNOWLEDGMENTS

SPECIAL EFFECT grew out of my love for the theater. "They" say "write what you know," and I've spent my life in the theater. So this tale is the result of my overactive imagination.

I thank so many people for helping bring the story to fruition. Among them are the talented writers of my writer's critique group: Varsha Bajaj, Kathy Duval, Linda Jackson, Marty Graham, and Vonna Carter. Special thanks to my multiaward-winning mentors, Kathi Appelt and Kelly Bennett. Kathi has been my champion for years, and Kelly has done countless readings of my manuscripts offering advice and sharing her vast knowledge of writing and publishing. I also offer special thanks to superagent Erin Murphy. Although she never signed me as a client, rejecting several of my early manuscripts and, indeed, the manuscript of *Special Effect,* she has always been supportive, and her critique of *Special Effect*, with specific suggestions, spurred me to revise, make it better, and get it to its present state.

And finally, I have so many friends and family who encourage me to write, are my sounding boards for ideas, and cheered me up when I felt that my work would never get acknowledged. First and foremost among those is my life partner and love, Jeffrey Greenwood.

PROLOGUE

I LOVE this theater. Sure, it's not in such a hot neighborhood. You have to fight off the junkies and whores just to get in the door, but it has history. The guy who built it was hot for an ancient movie called *The Hunchback of Notre Dame*. Well, I guess it was a *new* movie when this baby was built. Anyway, the star of that movie was Charles Laughton, hence the name of the theater: the Laughton.

I can almost hear a *hiss-s-s-s* as I push the stage door shut. This old gal—as my friend Zach calls the place—has a bunch of hideous medieval monstrosities, a gaggle of gargoyles, lining the walls of the auditorium. They used to scare the crap out of me when I came in. I'd throw the deadbolt on the stage door, then flip the switch next to the door. The stage would flood with light, but the seating area would glow dimly in the spill. That's when the gargoyles shine.

You see, someone washed 'em with bright-colored paint. It's always been that way, I was told. When I first started working here, I'd forget, and then I'd turn around and just about jump out of my skin because those things were glaring at me.

Fat chance that anyone else would be staring at me. You see, at the time this happened, I was that rare seventeen-year-old guy who couldn't seem to make a connection—by that I mean *get a date*. As much as I love theater, I probably volunteered here at the Laughton because I didn't have anything else to do. It's not like someone was knocking down my door to whisk me away for a romantic evening of fun and frolic.

No, I could count my friends on one hand—and most were the "at school" kind, not the "let's go to a movie" kind or "let's kick it at Mickey D's" kind. You know, you're friendly at school, but as soon as the final bell rings, no one ever calls you. And that just makes it harder for you to call them.

Made me a loner. Or maybe that should read *loser*. Alone with no one knocking on my door begging me to be their friend.

I suppose you might say that the only true friends I had, I met at this theater. None of 'em my age, but friends nonetheless. They make me feel like… like I've got some special talent. And maybe I do. Working here takes me out of that lost place, that place where I just try to get through the day. That place called *school.* Here, I just kick back, do my job, and enjoy being with my true friends.

Until recently, though, none of those had offered me the least bit of romantic inclination.

I'm Nick, by the way… Nick Fortunati. Ironic name, huh? That's Italian for *lucky people.* You may have figured that out, or at least knew it has something to do with good luck. But fortune had never smiled on me. Yes, I come from this big Italian family—how my folks got away with having only one kid, I'll never understand—who are always surrounded by other family members, friends of family members, and friends of friends. And believe me, they are all—at least, the ones who are my age or older—either married, engaged, or dating. That left me… the loner. It was like I was adopted from some hermit couple. But, you see, there was a reason why I couldn't seem to find someone. And it is a reason that will become clear very soon in this story I need to tell. And lest you think this is a depressing tale, let me spell it out for you right up front. Before this, I was one of those people who is on the outside looking in, never really living life. But this, this *experience*, taught me. I've learned a lot during the course of all this. So be patient.

Because this is one strange story. I'd bet you've never heard anything like it. And I'd also bet you won't believe it. I sure wouldn't if it hadn't happened to me. But let me tell you, this creepy old place is the perfect setting for what I'm about to relate.

It all began one Saturday morning….

CHAPTER 1

"HEY, NICK! You already here? When I said Saturday morning, I didn't mean the crack of dawn, son."

Zach Provost came down the aisle of the theater. Zach is about the coolest guy I know: by day, one of our city's leading architects; by night, a wizard who creates dazzling lighting effects for the Streetwise Players, one of the best community theaters in our state. And I, my friends, am the assistant to this genius.

"There's no overtime pay here for being early," Zach quipped.

"Har-de-har-har-har," I shot back, doing my best Three Stooges imitation. "I haven't seen a paycheck yet, and I've been working here about a year now, *Dad*."

"That's why they call it community theater, son. And don't call me Dad."

"Why not? You call me *son* all the time." I shook his hand as he came on the stage.

"Yeah, well, that's one of my bad habits. The wife says I do it just because I can't remember the names of my four sons, but that's not true. There's Sammy, Jimmy, Trent, and... uh-h-h—" He put his finger to his nose, scrunched his eyes, and nodded his head rapidly, like some thought was trying desperately to break into his consciousness. "—what's his name... the little one with the bad cowlick."

"Good one, Zach, good one," I said, laughing.

That's what I like about Zach. He has a wicked sense of humor. You're probably thinking, Zach is just a substitute for my own, abusive, wigged-out, absent father. Not true. I've got the best dad anybody could ever have. Even if we don't always see eye to eye.

But I have to admit, Zach sees something in me that my dad doesn't see. My dad has a plan for my life. He's blinded by his grandiose scheme. Doesn't know or care about what I want. I love him, but geez. Sometimes I feel like my dad is no different from all those kids at school who see right through me like I'm invisible.

"So," Zach said, "you ready to work? I've got the light plot right here. Let's sit, and I'll walk you through it."

We went down the three steps off the stage and settled into a couple of choice seats. Zach pulled a folded sheet of paper from a folder he'd been carrying and flipped it out in front of me.

"Impressive," I said.

"Yeah, that's what you adoring apprentices always say." Zach nudged me with his shoulder. "You guys always want to kiss up to us important people."

I just shook my head. "Delusional." I sighed.

"*What*? You don't think the Streetwise Players is lucky to have me?" He laughed.

"Yes, I do," I said, seriously. "But enough of this… talk me through this plot."

Zach had drawn a detailed diagram of what lighting instruments we would be using and where each one would hang. It was a fairly standard plot for the set—an English drawing room. The show was one of those "Colonel Mustard in the drawing room with the candlestick" type of murder mysteries. The only unusual thing was the last scene, where the ghost of the victim rose up to heaven, having been avenged.

Yeah, I know, *what a crock*, you say. But the Streetwise audience would eat it up. They come here in their Beemers, Jags, and Benzes for a night of mindless entertainment, and that's what we give 'em. In return, the glitterati of our fair city have made this one of the most successful community theaters in the nation. We may provide the talent, but they provide the capital… shows are almost always sold out.

Too bad they don't do more than buy tickets. Yes, the ticket sales keep us afloat, or so I'm told, but if more of them would donate some of their millions, we could fix up this old place. The Players got the Laughton for a song, and it's pretty much stayed the same in the ten years they've had it.

Proceeds from ticket sales are plowed right back into production, which means the shows are great, and—more important to our audience—security in the parking lot is super tight. We take care of our patrons.

"The plot is just general lighting," Zach said, pointing to his diagram. "You'll need six Fresnels on the first batten, six on the second, six on the third. The scoops are already hung from the last show. And, here"—he jabbed at the drawing—"you'll need a Leko with a blue gel."

Now, before you get all weirded out with the theater lingo, all you really need to know is that Fresnels blend, scoops flood, and Lekos spot. Lights, get it? But we call 'em lamps, and don't get 'em confused with the lamp on your mom's living room table. Oh—it's important to this show that you know a Leko is like a special spotlight.

"You want the Leko on the first pipe or the second?" I asked, staring up at the battens—pipes where we hung the lamps.

"It's all here in the plot, son." Zach grabbed my head, pulled it down, and pushed it to the diagram.

"You mind if I breathe while I look at this?" I fake-gasped.

He released his hand from the back of my head.

"Oh yeah, now I see… the first pipe."

"Yep," he said, "if we focus it right and use the special effect I've concocted, it will look just like a wisp of gray smoke rising to heaven. I'm hoping for a collective gasp from the audience as that ghost meets his reward."

"You da man, man." I punched him on the shoulder.

"Thank yew. Thank yew very much." He used his best Elvis impersonation.

"Elvis has left the building, Provost. Let's keep him that way." I bopped him one, and he laughed. It's fun to joke around, like equals. After all, I graduate soon. My dad still treats me like I'm thirteen. Zach, though, he's different.

"Man, it's been a crazy week," he said, rubbing his eyes. "My job has kept me jumping; plus I had to do this brilliant plot here."

"Poor wittle Zach, him's all tired from workin' so hard," I teased.

"Yeah, well, you just try to work, do all this stuff here, and keep up an active social life, thanks to my lovely social-butterfly wife."

"Well, I do have full-time school, and I work here all the time, so I could use a little sympathy too, you know."

"Right, son," he said. Then he held up his fingers and wiggled them at me, chanting, "Sympathy, sympathy, sympathy."

"You're a cruel man, Zach Provost."

"But you know you love me." He laughed again. "So you mentioned school and work here, but you left out the third element. How's your love life?"

I almost choked. Zach really did think he was my dad or something. Only my dad would never have come up with that question. I don't think he even gives a thought to the fact that I don't date. Maybe it's because I'm never home. I'm always here at the Laughton.

"We-e-e-l-l," I drawled as I searched for an answer. Oh sure, I could have spilled my guts to him, but really? Wouldn't that be disgusting and degrading? Finally I blurted out, "Pretty much nonexistent. How's yours?"

"You may have heard—I'm off the market, son… prized wife and four utterly charming rug rats. I'm taken, but you—you're young and virile. There must be someone you have your eye on."

"Uh-uh. No one I'm eyeing, and no one eyeing me. Simple truth."

"Well, you just keep your options open. Someone'll fall in your lap. You're a catch, son, a real catch."

Now, if any other person my parents' age had said that to me, I would have felt weird, icky all over, you know what I mean? But Zach? He's different. It's like he cares about me and wants me to find someone.

He laughed. "Okay, now, you think you can pull all these and get 'em hung?"

"Aren't you going to help me?" I whined—but he knew I was quite happy working by myself.

"Nah, son, you're on your own. Robbie has a soccer game, and Diane'll kill me if I miss it." He stood, and I did too.

Diane is the aforementioned wife, and Robbie is that son he'd pretended not to remember.

"Well," I said, "head on out, because I don't want your boys having to spend their inheritance on a lawyer for their mom's defense."

Zach smiled as he pointed at me. "That's a good one. See ya."

And he vanished into the lobby.

I spent a few minutes studying the plot Zach'd left. Then I headed to the storage room stage left, thinking of Zach. He really was brilliant when it came to stage lighting. And he really meant it when he asked me those personal questions. He cared. If only I could come clean with him. I'd bet he'd understand, but it would be a risk. A big risk.

Someone had piled a bunch of paint cans right in front of the door to our storage. That's the thing about community theater. We're all volunteers, and some of us aren't the brightest lights in the galaxy. I would have thought *hey, somebody might need to get in this storage room before I get back for more painting,* but that's just me.

I pulled out my master key—I'm one of the few volunteers around here who has one—and slipped it in the lock. After I turned it, I pulled on the door, dragging the paint cans along with it. I know, you're most likely thinking *why not move the cans?* Well, that would just take time and energy, which I could better spend on the job at hand.

While I slid the key into my pocket, I smiled as I remembered what Zach had said when he'd given it to me: "Look, son, not many of our workers are trusted with one of these—especially not the ones like you, of the teenage persuasion. You better not lose it and make me look bad."

Like I would ever do that. That's the last thing I would want to do to Zach. And, besides, I'm nothing if not trustworthy. Or anal, if you want to think of it that way. When I'm here, I'm constantly worried about where the key is; when I'm not here, I keep it hidden in my car. Anal? Paranoid? Trustworthy? Maybe all three. Or maybe just afraid of disappointing Zach.

I pulled the door open only enough for me to get through. I reached for the light switch and flipped it. Nothing happened. I shuddered. *Why can't they keep a working lightbulb in here?* It seemed like every time I needed something out of this storage room, the bulb was burned out. I guess it must be the old wiring in this place. Well, I would just have to do this in the semidarkness, I decided. Thank God, I could figure out Fresnels from Lekos in the dark. And thank Dionysius, I'm not afraid of the dark. It can get pretty creepy around here. And, in case you're wondering, Dionysius is the god of the theater. I'm a theater nerd, what can I say?

I stepped over to the pipe where the Fresnels were usually hung. I reached for the wrench I had slipped into my back pocket and started to loosen the bolt around the pipe.

"Need some help?"

I whipped around, jumping at this voice out of nowhere. What was that I said about not being afraid of the dark? I about jumped out of my skin. I'd thought I was alone.

A shadowy figure blocked the doorway.

"Who the hell are you?" I spat.

CHAPTER 2

THE FIGURE backed off a few steps as I moved toward the door but was still in shadows. He put his hands up defensively. *At least it's not a ghost*, I said to myself, chuckling inside to let off the pent-up steam of being startled. I couldn't tell for sure, but from the size and shape, I was reasonably certain it was a man. Strung-out junkie/helpless lighting technician scenarios flashed through my mind.

"Whoa," he said. "I don't want no trouble here. I just thought you could use some help." And he backed a few steps farther.

My first instinct, because of the neighborhood we were in, was to lock myself in the storage room, but then I thought, *Oh yeah... that would be smart. Then he'd have you cornered, could break down the door, and beat you to a bloody pulp.*

So I crept into the light, pushing my glasses up my nose so I could focus better. They'd slipped down when I jumped. I guess I really was startled by this guy.

I could see he was a kid about my age. He was definitely an individual, but he didn't look dangerous—not like the homeless druggies who prowled the streets outside. I sniffed. He didn't smell like one of them, either. No, this guy was clean, even though he had the goth thing going on... dressed all in black. He had long blond hair and a taut, swimmer's body. Good-looking guy.

"How'd you get in here?" I asked. I was careful to keep my fear in check, to refrain from letting him get the upper hand if he was indeed a threat.

"Hey, take a chill pill, dude. I'm here all the time. This place is home to me."

Take a chill pill? What? Is this guy into retro? "Dude"? Didn't that word go out with the eighties? Weird.

He just stood there, staring at me.

I eyed him back. It pissed me off to find out that Streetwise had trusted another volunteer my age with a key too. But that had to be the case. How else could he have gotten in?

"I didn't mean to freak you out." He backed even farther away, like he was as uncertain of me as I was of him. "I just saw that you were fixin' to work with the lights. I've done a lot with lighting here, so I thought you could use some help. But, hey, if you don't want any help, that's cool."

"You work here? What crews have you been on? You haven't done lighting crew while I've been here." I tried to keep my voice even. I wanted to scope out the guy without tipping him off that I was fishing for info about him. I had to find out if he was really a threat, either to my physical well-being or to my position here at Streetwise. Frightened? A little. Jealous? A lot.

"I've done most everything around here, from swabbing out the dressing rooms to ticket sales."

Ticket sales? If he'd worked ticket sales, that meant he *had* been around a lot longer than me. *I* hadn't gotten to handle money yet.

"But what I like most is the lights. They're like, bodacious, man."

I liked his enthusiasm, but I still had to wonder if he spent his nights watching MTV from twenty-five years ago. *Bodacious?*

"What's your name, bro?"

"Steve Stripling," he answered.

"You go to school around here?" I asked.

"Used to. St. Pius."

"What? You graduate?"

"Yeah. But that seems like a long time ago."

"Last year, huh?" He just stared at me. "Well, I'm a senior at Dulles, so it looks like you're a year ahead of me."

There was something about the guy.... I don't know. He was strange, a little out of sync, but I just got a gut feeling that he was, you know, one of the good ones, that I could trust him. Come on. I know you're thinking I'm a fool. But really, this Steve guy simply didn't seem like someone to be concerned about. And I like to think I'm a pretty good judge of character. Or maybe I was just desperate for a friend my age.

"I know just about everything there is to know about the lights here," he volunteered. What? If he was a lighting guru, then why hadn't I met him before? That should have been a red flag, right there. But I wanted to get to know the guy better, and working together is the best way to get to know someone.

"Great," I said. "Let's get started, then. I've got to hang the upcoming show, and since tech week is coming up, I need to get the job done today. You up to doing a little grunt work?"

"I'm amped. What do you want me to do?"

"I was just about to pull lamps from storage."

"Don't you think it would be easier if these went away?" Steve pointed to the paint cans.

"Yeah, you're right. I was just being lazy, but if you could move 'em, it would be a big help, okay?"

"You got it." He immediately set to work while I inched back into the storage room. Good start. The guy didn't mind grunt work. I liked that about him. If he was here to help, then I expected him to do it with a smile.

"Tech week, huh?" Steve huffed and puffed from outside the door as he carted the cans away. Really was grunt work, I guess. "We used to call it Hell Week. There's nothing worse than the week spent setting a new show."

"Don't I know it," I shouted back. "Just when you think everything is perfect, the director changes it all. Then it's back to the drawing board. Definitely Hell Week." I kicked the door open and set two Fresnels outside the door. "Take these out to center stage, will you? I'll pull some more."

When I set two more outside the door, Steve was waiting to haul those off. We continued that assembly line until all the lamps were pulled and ready to hang. Having a helper sure made the job go quicker.

And besides, it felt good just to have another guy around my age. Knowing Steve might lead to something, you know. Or he might hook me up with someone. I was beginning to like my prospects here.

I had worked up a sweat, even with Steve's help. I took off my glasses, wiped the bridge of my nose, then put them back on. That simple act nagged at me a moment. I usually don't wear my glasses when I'm around strangers. Glasses suck. Or, at least, I think I look sucky in them. I've had mine since I was seven. And I've always thought that people automatically think you're weak or dumb or something if you wear glasses as thick as mine. But I have no choice. I'm blind as a bat—really, I can't see more than two feet in front of me without 'em. I like to ease into my nerd look with new people, especially with another guy like Steve. If I know that a new guy is around, I slip 'em off, then after we talk awhile, I take my glasses out of my pocket, clean 'em a bit, then casually slip them on, tossing off something like, "Being blind's a bitch." Another weird quirk of mine, I guess, to go with all the rest that makes up loner/loser Nick: no glasses around strangers. But I had forgotten I was wearing them (seeing clearly can do that to you), so I guessed the cat was out of the bag.

Steve was different, though. He didn't blink at my thick specs, he jumped right in to help, and he worked as hard as I did. My kind of guy.

"Now," I said, "the fun part. Let down the first pipe, would you?"

He bounded over to the rail, unclamped the rope for the first pipe, and, thanks to the magic of counterweights, the pipe came down toward me. He clamped it off just at chest level, perfect for attaching the lamps.

With that simple task, Steve proved himself. Only someone who had done lighting would have known the perfect height for the pipe. He did it like a pro. I still wondered why we'd never worked together before, but maybe it was because he was box office. I was usually cocooned in the light booth.

Together we secured the Fresnels on the first pipe, then started on the second.

"I have to tell you—I'm likin' having help here. Usually, I'm all alone… just me and the gargoyles."

Steve laughed. "Creep you out, huh?" he said.

"Nah, man. I like 'em. They got character... especially with all that bright-colored paint on 'em. Who in hell ever thought to paint 'em like that, I wonder."

"The strippers did it," Steve said.

"Strippers?" That was a new one to me. Nobody at Streetwise had ever mentioned strippers before. Steve was proving to be quite an eye-opener.

"Yeah. Before this theater company took over, this place was kickin' with strippers."

I looked at him. "I thought it was empty before we bought it."

"It was—for about ten years. The gals were before that."

"Really?"

"Only they didn't call themselves strippers. They preferred *exotic dancers.*"

"How do you know all this?" I asked.

"Palace of Exotic Dance... that's what they called the place. Did you ever hear of burlesque?"

"Lots of bad comedy and girls with their tits showing?" I read a lot of theater history. It's kind of a hobby of mine. You spend a lot of time by yourself, you need a hobby. "But that was a long time ago."

"Sure was. And the Palace here featured burlesque long after the rest of the world had kicked it to the curb."

"Amazing. I wonder if the Streetwise board of directors knows about this. They could do a 'look back into history' show. I can just see the theater president, Tina Silver, with her tits hanging out."

"I don't know which one she is. She a honey?" Didn't know Tina Silver. And he did ticket sales. I'd figured Silver kept her hand on the till very, very tightly. I guess not. Maybe that's why we have a treasurer, but Silver does run everything around here.

"Oh yeah," I deadpanned, "she's smokin'. She's about ninety years old, fifty-pound bags under her eyes, and hair so bleached that it glows in the dark."

"H-m-m-m... babe-o-rama."

I liked this guy. We seemed to have the same sense of humor.

Steve helped me install the lamps on the third pipe; then I said, "Hand me that Leko, will ya?"

Hoisting up the heavy lamp, Steve said, "What's this for?"

"A special." I hummed an eerie tune from some old TV show. "Ghost… woo-woo." I waved my arms in the air, wiggling my fingers, a blank stare on my face. "This baby will light the special effect that our esteemed lighting director Zach has created—the ghost, having been avenged, rises to heaven."

"It's not like that, you know. Ghosts don't rise into heaven."

I clamped the Leko on the pipe.

"Whatever." I shrugged. "Our audiences will eat it up." As I tightened the clamp, I thought I heard the lobby door screech. I tested the clamp to make sure it was tight. You don't want an instrument falling on an actor's head. No one came in, so I guessed I was just imagining the sound.

"Hand me that blue gel." Plugging in the lamp, I reached back for Steve to hand me the piece of blue-colored filter I was going to put on the lamp. I waited a few seconds, then said, "The gel?"

Still nothing.

I turned around.

"What the…?" Steve was gone, vanished without a word.

CHAPTER 3

I WAS thinking 'bout Steve when I sat down at Koffee Kart—man, I love those dolce lattes.

But I digress.

What had made Steve bolt out of there like that? Had I been bossing him around? Had he suddenly remembered he had a dentist's appointment? What? The way he talked, maybe he'd needed to catch the train back to the eighties.

Then I laughed to myself.

A weirdo and a half. Maybe I should have been glad he skated. I liked him and all, but there was something very strange about him.

After removing the lid from my coffee and taking a big bite of the coffee cake I'd bought, I opened up my laptop.

Now, here's the 411 about Koffee Kart. They're all over our town. Started out as one lone little place, then they just took off. There are more KKs here than Starbucks. Great coffee and free Wi-Fi. Beats corporate coffee any day.

I looked around, making sure no one was looming over my shoulder. I was the only customer in the place, thank God. I was in stealth mode. For a reason. A good reason. This KK is not far from my school.

Then I booted up and clicked on Internet Explorer. I went to Favorites and called up my favorite site: Metropolitan Gay Youth

Alliance. Under that, a menu appeared: Home, Our Mission, Activities, How to Join, Where to Find Us, Contact Us.

Pushing my glasses up my nose, I pointed the mouse to Our Mission and read the statement: *Metropolitan Gay Youth Alliance was founded to be a safe haven for the gay youth of our area. Led by caring gay and lesbian adults—and with certified counselors available— MGYA offers social activities in a relaxing setting where gay and lesbian teens can interact with each other without fear or threat from a homophobic world. We realize that we all must learn to live in a world that is less than accepting sometimes, but MGYA provides a place where youth can escape for a while and develop social skills that can help them cope with a harsher reality that they face daily.*

I bet I've read that about a thousand times. One of these days, it might just give me the courage to go to a meeting. Chickenshit. Not you, me.

Meanwhile, I clicked on Activities. Pics of pairs of boys, pairs of girls, all having fun. They played pool; they hiked. There was a shot of a group outside a movie theater. And then there was the one I liked the most: dressed up in formal clothes, same-sex couples were slow dancing. The caption read Our Annual Senior Prom.

Damn, damn, damn. I slipped my cup off the napkin it was on to wipe my cheek.

I didn't need to click on How to Join because I knew how. It was simple. Just show up at a meeting. So simple, yet so hard.

Another cheek swipe. Happened every time. I don't know why I called up this site there, in public. Anybody could see me getting all teary. But there's no lock on my door at home. Safer to call it up here than there.

I looked back at the screen.

God knows, I didn't need the Where to Find Us map. You see, here's the deal—the place is right next to my dad's office. Uh-huh… if I go there, Dad is pretty likely to see me there. Getting the picture?

Remember I told you I had the best dad in the world… except…?

You're thinking it was the planning my whole career thing, aren't you? No, it was bigger than that.

It was a huge, enormous, gigantic exception. My dad is not, shall we say, *enchanted* with queers. That's his word, not mine.

The way I hear it, Dad's best friend in college was gay. But he made the mistake of coming on to Dad, who freaked out. My dad, who could stay calm in a typhoon, went ballistic when his best friend touched him. Ever since then, he's been homophobic. I mean big-time.

It's like if your neighbor's Chihuahua bites you, and ever after, you quiver whenever a little dog comes around.

So now you know why I'd never dated. And that, of course, also meant no sex. Yeah—I know I could have been the brave activist, defied Dad, and all that shit. But I didn't have that kind of courage. So, it was easier just to stay in the deep, dark closet, not letting anyone know that I was the big old gay I am. Still, I did *wish* sometimes. *All the time.*

But enough about that—I had bigger problems. Of the planning-my-career kind.

You see, Dad's company—Dad's a biotech process engineer— funds a scholarship each year at our local hallowed institute of higher learning, Crevette University, founded in 1867 by our own rich-as-Croesus billionaire John Monroe Crevette, railroad tycoon. And, wouldn't you know it? The good son that I am, qualified for the company's scholarship. I *had* to get As in physics, huh?

Now, I'm not knocking Dad's job—he loves it—but picture this: he spends all day supervising a staff doing some sort of experiments in purification techniques. If you're nodding off right now, then you know exactly how I feel. That is the farthest thing from the excitement of creating theater.

But, being the *good little son*, I was stuck.

Dad made me apply. I tried to talk him out of it, but this was his argument: "What? Do you think I'm made of money? This is your free ride, kid."

Me: But Dad, I don't want to be a bioengineer. I want to major in theater.

Him: Theater? You mean with all the queers? Uh-huh, not my boy. It's bad enough you hang around with those pansies at that community theater." (Like he'd ever been there.) "But you're not going to spend your whole life in that world. No way. You'll get this scholarship, get a great job, and then you'll be able to support that sweet little wife you'll have one day. I want me some grandkids, bucko."

Dad can be a pain too. Great dad, but at times, a great pain. Throwback to the fifties. Mom stands up to him. I can just hear her: "Sweet little wife? That what you think of *me*? Apron, broom, and cookbook in hand? Leave the boy alone." But she won't go any further than that. She loves keeping the peace, and if letting Dad run my life means a happy home, then she is not about to fight for me.

Maybe I should talk to Mom, get her to fight for me, but in the end, it's my battle.

But when Dad says *bucko*, I know the argument is over. He never uses the word unless he is *closing the subject*. Grandpa says it all the time, so I guess that's where Dad got it from.

So, now you see my dilemma. It sucks.

So, there I sat, mooning over this website like some sick cow.

I slammed shut my laptop. Why keep looking at it when I was such a wimp? I could put on my big boy pants and just go to a meeting, but no—I didn't have the balls to do that. All I could do was sit here, staring at a computer screen.

I took a swig of my coffee and stared out the window. A kid passed on the sidewalk. He was all in black.

Oh my God. It's him.

Then the guy glanced toward the window. Not Steve.

My heart dropped. Reality bites. At that moment, I realized why I'd accepted Steve so easily. I didn't know him. Didn't really even learn anything about him in the short time we'd worked together. It all boiled down to one thing: I wanted him. I was horny as hell, didn't know how to do anything about it, and what's more, I had let him get away.

I wished it had been Steve outside that window. He might have been strange, but he was a looker. I'm a sucker for curls, man. And that long blond hair of Steve's had curls that fell all around his emerald-green eyes and delicious pink lips.

Am I a romance novel waiting to happen or what?

As I knocked back my latte, I got a warm feeling all over, and it wasn't from the coffee. I was really, really *wanting* Steve. Sometimes you just want to be held, to be touched. And *sometimes....*

That's when it hit me. Dad never, ever sets foot in the Laughton Theater, and, seeing as how I spent so much time there, something might come of this Steve thing.

That was if Steve came back. And if Steve was gay. And those were two big ifs.

Two big ifs that were making my heart race.

Now, before you think I'm some kind of pervert who is only interested in booty, let me spell it out. I want the same thing all of you do. But it's easier if a guy is interested in girls. You can strike up a friendship, go on dates, go to her house, meet her folks, kiss her in public, hold hands, and then, if things happen, then things happen.

We're not like that. Gays have made a lot of progress these days, but teenage gays? Not much. We're still looked down upon, picked on, harassed. You know who you are. And it's not like I don't understand why you do it. I just wish you'd let up. We all just want the same thing, right? L-O-V-E... does that spell it out for you? We all just want to be cared about.

And if you have a Dad like mine, well, I *really* get it. It—that hatred—gets ingrained in you, you know. It's like my great-grandma on my mom's side. She grew up hating black people. Great-Gran is the sweetest, most loving person in the world, 'cept for that one blind spot. She just doesn't see the person. All she sees is the color.

So think twice the next time you see *one of us*.

Lecture over. Period. Now, what was I talking about?

Oh yeah... the cute curls, the green eyes, the pink lips.... Shit. You got it—*it* was happening again.

I had to get out of there.

CHAPTER 4

"JUST A smidge to the right, Nick... there. Perfect!" Zach shouted directions from the center section. He sat about three-quarters of the way up from the apron of the stage, supervising while I was perched on the twelve-foot ladder, focusing the lights.

I was bathed in "moonlight," adjusting the Special over the staircase. Minilecture alert—in case you weren't paying attention when I said it before: a Special is what we call the lamp we use for a special effect. Aren't you glad I believe in education? You could be sitting here totally in the dark. Get it? In the dark? Stop me before I wet my pants. I'm so funny—not.

"Lord, I'm brilliant. That ghost effect will blow everyone away," Zach yelled.

What a way to spend a Sunday afternoon... working in a dark theater with an egomaniac.

"Hey, I know you designed this," I yelled, "but don't I get some credit for climbing this ladder?"

Zach laughed. "Okay, I guess the grunts, not just the geniuses, need positive strokes too." Zach intoned, "Thank you, kind assistant and lighting god, for your expert tech work up there in the heavens."

"Don't mock me, old man."

"What?" he said, his voice all hurt and innocence. "You're the one who demanded affirmation from the master." He chuckled.

Zach might be an egomaniac, but he's a likeable egomaniac.

Then he shouted, "Now, get your butt down from there and come out here to see your handiwork."

I hopped off the ladder, took the apron steps, bounded up the aisle, and plopped down next to Zach.

"Sweet," I said.

"*Sweet*? Sweet, you say?" Zach was on a roll. "How about awesome? Brilliant? Stupendous? Show some love here, son."

"You did a fine job, sir," I deadpanned.

"I'm docking your pay. And there'll be no gruel for you tonight." He bopped me on the head.

"Please, sir, I want some more." I held up an imaginary bowl and used my best Cockney accent. And in case you don't get the joke, it's a line from *Oliver!,* a musical the Players did last season.

"Okay, man... it's a wicked effect." This time I was being serious. I can only razz Zach for so long before I realize he uses quips to fish for affirmation. We all need approval, huh?

"Thank you," he said.

We sat a few minutes in silence. I love my dad, but I think having a cool dad like Zach would be nice too. I always get the feeling that somehow he *knows* about me and approves. Wishful thinking, maybe.

"So, how's school?" he asked. "You spend so much time here. I don't want your schoolwork to suffer."

A real dad, didn't I tell you?

"I've got a 3.9. In fact, if the valedictorian hadn't taken so many home ec courses, I'd be way ahead of her. But salutatorian is okay with me." In fact, I'm pretty proud of my accomplishments, but I didn't want to sound too conceited. And besides, time spent apart from the crowd is time that can be spent studying.

"Wow, I guess I needn't worry about you anymore, scholar. And that love life thing? Any progress?"

Do I tell him, or don't I? That's what I was thinking. Zach would understand. Hell, I was reasonably certain he already knew, right? But... but.... Chickenshit.... Pantywaist.... I kept quiet.

"Still nil. You keep me hopping around here. Who has time for anything else?" I clasped my hand to my heart. "I'm just a slave to stage lighting."

Zach laughed and bopped me again.

"Hey, did you hear about the *Tribune* story?" He changed the subject.

"What? I ain't heard nothin'."

"3.9, huh?" He rolled his eyes.

"Yep, I lost me some a them there points in Ainglish class…. So, tell me about the *Tribune* thing."

"A reporter from the *Trib* is doing a story on the Laughton. Silver asked me to research a little and give him an interview. So I went through all those boxes stored in the office. Interesting stuff."

"Like what? Don't leave me hanging, here." I really did want to know more, especially about the strip joint.

"Well, okay, here goes… the first owner named the place after the actor in *Hunchback*."

I nodded.

"So—it was one of those grand movie palaces for thirty-odd years. Then a different kind of show took over."

"The strippers, right?"

"Well now, you've spoiled my story. Who told you about the strippers?"

"Steve did," I said.

"Steve? Who's he?"

"You know. The kid who dresses in black. 'Bout my age."

Zach bit his tongue and scrunched up his face, like he was thinking.

"Nope. I don't know any Steve."

That seemed odd. Sooner or later, you run into just about everyone around here.

Zach continued, "Then again, I don't know all the volunteers around here. He's never worked lights, though, I can tell you that."

"But he said he liked working lights the best. Come on, Zach… blond, curly hair, green eyes."

"Must have been before my time. Diane and I only moved to town two years ago." I thought Zach had been around here for ages. "Maybe that Steve kid worked with Hanks." Hanks was Mick Hanks,

Zach's predecessor. Zach shrugged. "Oh well, what were we talking about?"

"The strip joint."

"Oh yeah." He paused. "Here's the good part. This place was owned by some low-level mafioso. Or, if you read the paperwork they left behind, it looks that way."

"Cool," I said.

"Cool? Yeah, if you're into illegal activities… guns, money laundering, drugs."

"Damn," I said.

"That's what I said when I read all that… mind-boggling stuff. But luckily that's all in the past. The neighborhood's a bitch, but the gentry is moving back, so we're sitting on a gold mine. And I'm glad that the gangsters changed out the light board before they left."

"They installed all those computers?" I said before I thought about it.

"Yeah, *3.9*, twenty-five years ago, a bunch of gangsters put in a state-of-the-art computerized lighting system… must have been a piece of cake for them, considering how advanced technology was in those days."

I hated it when he did that—made me feel like a fool. Okay, okay, okay, I hear you… when *I* made me feel like a fool.

"No, son, *we* put in all the computers. But at least the previous tenants wired us up for all that, somewhat. The original controls were big levers. You know that locked closet thing just by the curtain at stage right?"

"Yeah," I said.

"Well, that's where they had all the old-fashioned dimmers."

Dimmers—make the lights fade in and out. End of lesson.

Zach continued his history lecture. "Okay, so the gangsters disconnected those old dimmers and installed a slide-type light board in the booth up there." He thumbed over his shoulder toward the control booth. Used to be the projection booth, in the old movie palace days. "I say the gangsters, because I have no idea who did it, but it happened on their watch. And, apparently, they padlocked the old control board door."

"You ever opened that thing?" I asked.

"Nah... never had any reason. Don't even have the key. Nobody here does." He stood. "Well, Diane wants me home for family night. You lock up, okay?"

"Sure. And thanks for the history lesson," I told him.

"I got kinda carried away, didn't I? The whole thing fascinates me."

Theater history. Another thing Zach and I have in common.

And he left.

I sat, admiring our handiwork. I love this place. And this show was going to be a big, big hit. There is nothing like the rush you get when a show is a smash.

I was lost in my work, just sitting there, when I felt a touch on my shoulder. Strange, though—I didn't jump. It was more like a warmth rather than a touch. Then I felt warm breath in my ear.

"I thought he'd never motor." I recognized that blond, curly, emeraldy, pouty voice. "Motor?" I looked up into those hovering green jewels.

"You know—*leave*."

Steve bounded over the seats and sat down next to me.

"Where'd you go yesterday, man?" I asked as he put his hand on my arm. I shuddered... a good shudder.

"Just needed to veg," he said, evasively. Then he brought his lips next to mine and gave me a soft, moist kiss. His breath steamed up my glasses.

"Whoa." I pushed him away. "What's going on here?"

"You don't like it?"

That stopped me. I yanked off my glasses and rubbed them with the tail of my shirt. I took a breath.

Here I was getting what I wanted. And it scared me.

"I do," I admitted, "but this is happening a little fast, don't you think?" *Stop it, Nick. Quit being an ass. You've wanted this forever. Maybe not with Steve—you just met him. But with someone.* It was a kiss, for Christ's sake. Just a kiss.

"Not *so* fast," he said. "I've been waiting a long time for this. And I've missed you. Yesterday was a long time ago."

So I had my answer. Wait, what was the question? My heart kept pounding. My mind kept racing. Beads of sweat popped out on my upper lip. I couldn't remember what I'd asked him.

He leaned in and locked his lips on mine again. This kiss lasted about five minutes, I think, and believe me, I was as hungry as he was. And this time I was ready.

But when he finally pulled away, I felt those old feelings tugging in me again. I was more confused than ever. It's tough being a newbie. In anything. But this? Deliver me, as Great-Gran would say.

You're thinking, *let it happen*, right?

But remember me? I was this guy who was too scared to even go to a meeting, you know?

"That was good."

Three tiny words. But in those three words, Steve set me at ease a tiny bit.

"I think I'm going to like this," he said. "Have you ever gone into something not knowing what the outcome would be, yet knowing that it was right, it was good?"

Was he saying he thought he loved me?

Dionysius! What do I do now?

"I've been waiting a long time for something like this to happen, for someone like you, Nick. I've been alone for so long, you know?"

No, I didn't know. And I wasn't sure about it all. You wait and wait for *life* to happen, then when it does, it scares the crap out of you.

Maybe this was just scooting by too fast.

CHAPTER 5

CUT TO the next night. I didn't see Steve. One night there, one night not.

After the night before, when we really didn't do much, I was sad—and maybe a little pissed—that he didn't show up again. I hate to say the word, but I guess I was a little lovesick. Or horny. Or both.

But I didn't have time to ponder the issue.

It was Hell Week at the theater. The last week before a show opens, everything has to come together—and more often than not, people are, as Great-Gran says, running around like chickens with their heads cut off. Costumers are still sewing on buttons (or worse, cutting out patterns). Actors are wishing they had memorized their lines two weeks earlier. Props people are still searching for that antique radio that is just perfect for the drawing room set. And lighting techs are incurring the wrath of directors who were too busy to meet with us to go over the plot and cues in detail before tech rehearsal. Get the picture?

Some directors are so blessedly organized that Hell Week transforms into Heaven Week. Some are so disorganized that you wonder how a show ever got put on. Legend has it that in the early days of the Streetwise Players, when they were bouncing from performance space to performance space, there was a director who was still building the set during Hell Week. The show was filled with special effects, so not only did the actors need a set to rehearse on; they needed to know how the effects were going to work. To add to the chaos, one of the supporting players had set-building experience, so instead of rehearsing, he was helping to construct. They say the show went up on time with white walls because there was no time to paint, effects that were untried, and a second lead who was shaky on his lines because he'd been building sets instead of his character. Now that's a bad director.

But the one we were working with was sort of in between. She was a tight-assed bitch who expected everything to be perfect on the first try. But perfection means a good show.

Even Mr. Nice-Guy Zach was ready to punch her lights out.

And adding to my misery was the mysterious Steve. Where was he? Last night he'd all but said he was in love with me. Yes, I freaked out over it, but after giving it some thought, I found I liked the idea— that maybe, just maybe, I was falling head over heels, too. Yeah, it seemed irrationally quick. But my being alone seemed to consume the last zillion years of my life. So I was ready for *quick*. And now he was nowhere to be found. Damn. All that talk about how *yesterday was a long time ago* and *it was good* and *waiting for something like this to happen* and he was MIA. Had I scared him off? That's all I needed.

And wouldn't you know it? That morning Dad started in about the scholarship thing. *The deadline's coming up, the deadline's coming up.* It was like he was a parrot who couldn't say anything else.

And I did something I never do. I got into it with him. All I said was, "Lighten up, Dad." That just set him off. Made me wish I'd kept my mouth shut.

But he knew me. He knew I'd make the deadline. I was salutatorian, for the love of Dionysius. You can't be a procrastinator and get that honor. I suppose valedictorian would have cinched Dad's precious scholarship, but he'd just have to deal.

Angry dad, anal director, absent Steve… it all just made it harder to concentrate on the show.

And crap. Wouldn't you know it? We got to the end of the show and the Special didn't work… that stupid "ghost" didn't rise to heaven after all.

Poor Zach. It was back to the drawing board for him. All I could think of was Steve's "ghosts aren't like that" or whatever the hell he'd said about the Special.

So, rehearsal was over and I wanted to hang back, hoping Steve would show up. After all, he'd seemed to like the theater deserted. But no such luck—the director "took a meeting" with Zach, so he told me to go on home.

On the drive home, I kicked myself over and over for not giving Steve my cell number the last time I'd seen him. Shit, what a screwup.

And—of course my luck, or lack of it, was holding—Dad was in his recliner, waiting. But he didn't look relaxed, no matter how stretched out he was. He wanted to talk to me.

"You send in that scholarship application yet?"

There was irritation in his voice as he popped the handle on the chair and jerked upright.

"I'll get to it. Have I ever let you down? Come on, cut me some slack here."

I was pushing my luck, but I'd had a bad day.

To his credit, Dad didn't say anything. He just sat there, glaring.

I talked fast. "I just have to arrange for another teacher to do a recommendation letter. Ms. Apley was absent today." I was stalling, and Dad probably could tell. But he didn't call me on my bluff. What he did was just plow right on, barking orders.

"Well, if Apley's not there tomorrow, go to someone else. You don't want to miss the deadline. Jim"—that's Jim Johnson, Dad's boss—"says you're a shoo-in. But he's getting antsy about you turning in that app. Friday will be here before you know it."

Remember how I told you I had the best dad in the world? I was rethinking that assessment. He could be so single-minded.

I went to bed that night and couldn't sleep. Who could? Just when I thought I could doze off, I'd think about four years spent getting a degree I didn't want. I'd turn over and vow to slumber; then the director's wrath would fill my head. She'd yelled at Zach, but it was my fault the effect hadn't worked. I must have rigged it wrong. I had to fix that problem. But how? Then I'd semibanish those thoughts from my head, and Steve's face would be there. Remembering the night before, I was beating myself up for his not being there tonight.

It was awful. You know how you have those sleepless nights, and then you can't stay awake, much less pay attention, in class the next day? That was me.

Next morning, in civics, I even fell asleep.

That would have been bad enough, but I woke up when my glasses clanked loudly as my head fell on the desktop.

"Mr. Fortunati." Ms. Apley's voice pierced my sleep-deprived haze. Oh boy—I knew I was in trouble. When a teacher calls you by your last name, unless it's PE class, it's not good. I quickly sat up, grabbed my pen, and tried desperately to look like I was hanging on her every word. "Can you elucidate for us how a bill becomes a law?"

Elucidate? Now she was just showing off. I hoped I could fake my way through the answer. The only thing was, after that, I had to ask her for that recommendation.

I opened my mouth to answer her question—what I was going to say, I didn't have a clue, but I had to come up with something, something that sounded vaguely like I had done my homework. I started to sputter an answer....

The bell rang. Literally, saved by the bell. I shuffled up to her desk, hoping I hadn't screwed up too bad by falling asleep in class. I *needed* her help.

"Ms. Apley?" I approached cautiously.

"Yes, Nick?" She looked up from her desk and smiled. It was a wicked smile that said "I caught you." If she'd been five years old, I might have seen her tongue pointed at me. Good. She was back to herself. The *Mr. Fortunati/elucidate* persona was gone.

"I'm applying for a scholarship at my dad's company, and I need a recommendation. Would you write one for me? The deadline is Friday. I could turn it in with my application. You could put it in a sealed envelope if you don't want me to see it." I rattled it all off quickly because we only have five minutes between classes, and Mr. Bohac, my next teacher, was a real hard-ass.

"Of course, Nick, no problem." Ms. Apley smiled. "Give me the information and I'll have it tomorrow."

"Thanks." I flashed a big smile as I handed her the info sheet and turned to go.

"Wait a minute." I turned back as she continued. "This says the scholarship is for bioengineering. What happened to your dream?"

Ms. Apley and her husband were Streetwise subscribers. She knew all about my work there. We frequently talked about the shows, picking them apart. She had a good eye for theater, and I'd learned a lot from our critique sessions.

"Lighting tech… professional theater?" she probed.

I looked down. "My dad thinks this would be better for me."

She strode over to me. "Nick, I'm not about to tell you to defy your dad. Dads usually do know what's best. But I am telling you that you two need to have a hard discussion. I can't picture you in a lab somewhere, pushing data around. Talk to him, Nick."

She was right. I should talk to him—without getting mad and spouting off. But she didn't know my dad. He gets something in his head and there's no changing him.

"Yes, ma'am. I will," I lied. "But meanwhile, can you just write that letter for me?"

She rolled her eyes and sighed. "I'll have it first thing tomorrow."

I spent the rest of the afternoon barely listening to anything in class. My mind raced with thoughts of Dad, Steve, the special effect. It was enough to make my head explode. I didn't know how to circumvent my dad's notions, I had scared off my first and only hope for a boyfriend, and my ass would be grass if I didn't get that effect to work before rehearsal. It was hard being me.

After a very long and exhausting day, the final bell rang, and I headed to my car. I had checked messages, and Zach had texted me to call him.

Zach picked up on the first ring.

"You rang, master?"

"Nick! Just the man I need. And please don't say no. That witch of a director has been calling me all day." I could hear the frustration in his voice.

"Say no to what?" I asked.

"Look—I think I figured out what went wrong last night with the Special."

"The timing was off," I said.

"Hey, I'm the lighting god here. Couldn't you have at least waited until I got it out?"

"Sorry, Zach. I'm dead tired. And I'm pretty sure my physics teacher caught me napping last period—my civics teacher sure did earlier—but before I nodded off, it came to me, and I know how to fix it. 'Kay?"

"You da man, *paisano*. I have a big presentation here that starts in ten minutes and will probably take until time for rehearsal tonight. So you get it done, son. I need you."

"Sure, Zach, anything you want."

"Great. Check you later."

I flipped my phone closed.

I started the engine and threw the car into reverse. I peeled out of the parking lot—after looking to make sure none of the faculty or security was spying—and made a left toward the Laughton.

When Zach says "jump," I always say, "how high?" Zach's praise breathes new life into me every time. And now, I had a burst of energy. I'd do anything for him.

Besides, I was headed to the theater anyway. Steve *had* to be there. I'd spent the whole day thinking about him, dreaming about him. Just ask my teachers. They could testify to how much I was out all day. And every nap included a Steve dream.

There was no way all that telepathy could be wasted. He would be there waiting for me. I knew it. After all, I'd figured out the special effect. Karma was emphatically in my corner today. Yes, Steve would be there.

And this time, I wasn't leaving without giving him my cell number. No way. No how.

The 'goyles hissed as usual when I shut the stage door. I threw on the work lights.

Then I made my way to the booth and booted up the computers. From the booth, I switched off the work lights and brought up the stage lights.

For about fifteen minutes, I fiddled with the sync of the effect until it was perfect.

I love my job. Using only lights, I get to create new worlds. Harsh worlds, happy worlds. Real worlds, fantasy worlds. I was so engrossed in my work that I didn't think of either of my other two problems. I just concentrated on my ghost.

I felt a draft as the door to the booth opened. I didn't have to turn around. I knew it was him.

"How you doin', lover?" He leaned over and gave me a peck on my neck.

I stayed cool. He'd totally ignored me the day before; I wasn't going to leap up and fall into his arms. I was worth more than that. If he couldn't work at this *whatever* we had, come around, care about us, then forget it. That's what I told myself, but it did take every bit of my resolve not to jump his bones. You see, inside I was hurting and pissed off, but oh, how good his caresses felt.

Steve sat in the chair next to me. For a moment, he was quiet. Was he actually contemplating my resistance to him? Well, he could just sit and stew if he thought I would come around so easily. I was better than that. I might have been horny and desperate, but I still had a shred of dignity. He could just mull over what was happening here.

Then he grabbed my cheeks in the palms of his hands, pulled me to him—so much for my resistance—and planted a big, juicy….

AARGH. Strike that. This is not a romance novel here. Suffice it to say, we kissed. And it was a good one. And my cool, detached resolve was shaken but not vanquished.

A good kiss didn't make up for what he'd done. I pulled away and sat, giving him my on-again silent treatment.

"Why so glum, chum?"

"Huh?" I said to him, shaking my head. What was up with his constant, annoying *ancient*-isms? "You've been watching too many *Leave It to Beaver* reruns." Even I could hear the annoyance in my voice. An annoyance that I felt but didn't want to express so strongly.

He laughed. "That's just something my mom used to say." Then he got quiet. The silence was palpable. It filled the tiny room with… what? Anguish? My heart started to melt. He seemed so sad. More than sad. I wanted to ask him why, but I sensed he might not want to talk about it. Besides, I was still mad at him.

"So—" He rubbed my arm. "—you gonna talk or not?"

"I'm about to drop, man. I couldn't sleep last night," I said, coolly. And truthfully. My newfound energy had drained, and I was feeling it.

"Why's that?" He put his hand on my shoulder and played with my ear. Shivers ran up my spine. It felt so good—not necessarily what he was doing, but just that someone was touching me in that way, you know what I mean? It was like—I don't know—healing and sexy at the same time. He had me. Oh, how just a little attention can melt you. And strange as it seems that I had such insight then, being a novice and all that, but it also felt like Steve, too, was crying out for closeness. The last time I'd seen him, he'd said he'd felt alone, now he was showing it somehow. He wasn't all good kisses. He wasn't just a horndog. He needed me as much I needed him.

"There's this scholarship my dad thinks I can get." He was turning me on, but I was still scared to do anything about it. This was all so new to me. And I have to admit, thinking about my dad at the same time was a bit of a joy killer.

"And that's a bad thing, how?" He almost whispered it in my ear. He was good. *He's done this before*, I thought. And that scared me even more. What if I didn't measure up?

His warm breath was making me crazy, but I kept talking, hoping to somehow sort all this out miraculously—my dad problems, my Steve dilemma.

"It's in bioengineering." I squirmed, feeling *it* grow. My strategy was *not* working. I kept trying. "I had planned to major in theater."

"Just tell your dad."

Easier said than done.

Steve licked my earlobe.

I pushed him away, laughing nervously. "Stop it. I'm going to explode here." My agitated giggle made me sound like a twelve-year-old girl.

He sat perfectly straight and still. "Yes, sir, sergeant, sir." He saluted me.

"You don't salute sergeants," I said, pushing his hand away from his forehead. The simple touch was electric. I wanted him. I was ready for him.

He looked at me with concern, not passion.

The *does Nick lose his cherry?* crisis was averted because Steve was now focused on my problem. I'm not sure I was happy about it, but it was what it was, and I *had* wished for it. Besides, his concern was nice. He wasn't all sweet kisses, it seemed. My problem had tapped into something deeper in him.

He was troubled. For me.

"So your dad's a hard-ass, huh?"

"Well, no... not normally. But this is one thing he won't budge on." And the gay thing, but *that* was definitely something I was not going to think of right then.

"So tell him no way—that you won't go to engineering school or med school or wherever it is those bio guys train." He was really into solving my problem now. It was a quality that was, as Great-Gran would say, *endearing.*

"I can't." *Once Dad finds out I'm gay, his bioengineering dream will be the only thing I have to stay in his good graces.* "If I miss the deadline for that scholarship app," I continued, "he'll kill me."

Steve thought a minute.

"So, go ahead and turn it in."

"But you're not listening, Steve—if I turn it in, I'm likely to win the scholarship. Then I'm doomed."

He shook his head.

"I'm just saying turn the app in. You don't have to take the scholarship."

"You're not making sense. Do you think my dad's going to let me turn down a full scholarship?"

"Probably not, but what if the scholarship you get offered is in theater?"

I rolled my eyes at him. He was being no help at all. "Yeah, yeah... I apply for a bio scholarship. They take one look at the app, smile, and say, 'We think we really want to send you to theater school. Is that okay with you?' What are you, Steve? Crazy?"

"Look, Nick. There's no law against turning in applications. You can fill out your dad's papers, you can fill out papers for the university theater. Who knows what might happen?"

"But what if there aren't any theater scholarships available?"

"Have you asked? Have you called them? Have you tried?" His voice rose with each question. Steve was getting excited at my prospects. "Contact the theater department over at Crevette. Find out if there is any cash available and how you can get it."

"And if I can get my own scholarship in theater, then Dad won't have anything to say about it if I turn down his thing."

"That's the ticket." He touched my cheek.

God, it felt good. There was passion in it; there was gentleness in it; there was love in it.

But I had to stay focused. We were solving my education problem right then.

"He'll be pissed, but I think he'd get over it." *Especially if I can keep the gay thing from him.* "Dad likes it when I take the initiative."

Steve grinned, and I melted.

I covered his hand with mine and looked into his eyes, moving in on him.

"Now, we've got two hours until rehearsal starts, and...."

I kissed his eyelids.

CHAPTER 6

"EVERYTHING LOOKS good here, Nick—may I call you Nick?" Max Nichols, the dean of the Crevette School of Theater, was looking over my paperwork.

I sat across from him, dressed in my best clothes—dark suit, conservative tie, dark socks (Mom is always griping about my white socks/dress clothes combination). I was even wearing my horn-rims. You know how I don't like to wear 'em when I first meet people? Well, I figured I needed to be able to see Dr. Nichols, so I kept 'em on. He wouldn't be too impressed if I stumbled all over his office, now would he?

When I'd gotten dressed that morning, it was a toss-up. Did I dress like a scholar or an artist? After all, it was a theater scholarship I was hoping for. I'd decided on scholar. I was dressed to impress.

I was, as they say on vocabulary lists, *exuding* confidence. I was the picture of *take me, I'm the best for the job*—or scholarship, that is.

"You have great recommendations from your teachers, a commendable grade point average, and a stellar letter from Zach Provost."

He smiled when he said Zach's name, like he knew Zach's work.

"That means a lot," he continued. "If the lighting man for Streetwise Players says we need you, then I'm all for it."

I grinned. I couldn't believe Zach had sealed the deal for me. Maybe he really was a lighting god.

"Does that mean I'm in?" I was in shock. This ball was rolling down the hill fast.

I had followed Steve's advice the next day. I arranged for a College Day—your school probably has something like it, but at our school, we can take a day off each year to visit colleges—and made an appointment with Nichols.

Now Nichols was telling me that I kicked ass. Could it have gone any easier?

"If it were totally up to me, yes, I would say you are in. But I have to run this by the acceptance committee. They make all the final decisions."

"But they listen to you, right?" I was hoping he would give me some more hope here.

"Yes, they listen, but they don't always rubber-stamp me." He put my papers back into a manila folder he had taken them from. "And, with a scholarship attached to this, it may be a little harder to push through. We have some excellent applicants this year."

"Look, Professor Nichols...." I stated my case once again. "I've learned an awful lot about lighting from Zach, I'm willing to learn a lot more, you've already said that you need a good lighting man, and I *need* this scholarship."

He smiled. "You're very persuasive, Nick. I like that. Shows initiative. Tell you what, I'll make sure you are accepted into the program. Then we can talk about a work-study program. It doesn't pay much, and you'd be busy all the time, but it could be your ticket here."

I stood up and offered my hand. "Thank you, thank you, thank you. I'm willing to work my butt... um—work until it kills me... to get this degree."

He laughed. "Well, our lighting man is a hard taskmaster. If he doesn't kill you, he'll make you stronger, as they say." He looked at his watch. "Now, I have a class to get to." He came from around his desk and put his hand on my shoulder. "You'll be hearing from me."

I was walking on clouds when I left Nichols's office. I was going to get in. Whoo-hoo. What more could I want? So what if I had to take the work-study thing? At least I would be in the theater program. I had to get to the Laughton to tell Steve—*if* he was there.

I ran to my car, got in, and started the engine. Then the brick to the forehead. You've probably already thought of this, but I was blinded by the work-study idea.

Would Dad think a work-study program was as good as a full ride? Not likely. Not even. What was I thinking? The only way I was going to avoid that white lab coat was if I could get a lighting scholarship. Nothing else would do.

I definitely needed to grow a pair where my dad was concerned, but I didn't know if that was gonna happen any time soon.

Which meant I had a secret. I couldn't tell Mom and Dad about the university. I could only tell Steve. The elusive Steve.

My mood was a lot darker as I drove to the theater. I hoped Steve was there. If I'd gotten his cell number, I could have called him. But we'd gotten a little *distracted*, if you remember, and phone numbers just never seemed to come up.

But as I opened the stage door, he was waiting for me. He gave me a bear hug and planted his signature juicy one on my lips. Then he noticed.

"Why so glum, chum?"

I didn't answer.

"You're scaring me, guy," he said. "Talk to me."

He followed me down the steps and into the seating. As I sat, I said, "I got a problem."

Steve jumped over the back of the seats and sat to my right. Then he said, "What? They don't want you at Crevette? I can't believe it." He stroked my arm, comforting me.

"Oh, that's not the problem. I talked to Professor Nichols, the head of the program, and he wants me there. He says that he will make it happen."

"So—why are you like, so bummed out, dude?" Steve took my hand in his.

He was doing all the right moves, saying all the soothing things, but I could only think of Dad, Dad, Dad.

"Because he made it pretty clear they won't have a scholarship for me. The only alternative is a work-study thing."

"That's not a bad idea. Work-study is better than nothing. You can do it. I know you can."

I wished I could believe him. I wished I could just let him take me in his arms and make it all better.

"Tell that to my dad. If I swing his company's scholarship—and Dad says I'm going to—then weigh a full ride against a work-study. It kinda tips the scales in Dad's direction, don't ya think?"

Steve wasn't having it. "Forget that. You'll be eighteen before long. Tell your dad to stuff it."

My stomach lurched at that suggestion. Remember that *pair* I needed to grow?

"I can't do that, Steve. You can't just say that to a man who has supported you your whole life. Would you do that to your dad?"

"I don't have a dad. But that's beside the point." He turned and looked at me. "It's your future we're talking about here. You can't blow it just because your dad has other plans for you." He ran the back of his fingers against my cheek.

Steve had just tossed off the comment about not having a dad. I wondered *what's up with that?* But I didn't ask because he was too engrossed in solving my problem, and that was endearing, as Gran would say. Steve more and more showed his love for me. And in showing how he felt and trying to convince me that I could stand up to my dad, he was making sense.

But I didn't know if I could do that to Dad or not. Maybe, in the back of my mind, I was thinking that if I was an engineer like he wanted, it would make things easier when I finally get the courage to come out to him. It's tough having two major obstacles in your path when it comes to your dad. Geez.

Have you ever had to tell your parents something you knew was going to hurt them? That's what I was facing. If things kept going good with Steve—and I really, really hoped they would—then I was going to have to tell my folks that I am gay. My mom might, and that's a big *might*, be okay with it, but you know how Dad would take it. If he hates me for turning down his precious scholarship, then think of how he'd feel knowing I'm gay. But, then again, if he already hated me, I guess it wouldn't matter.

I was so confused. And Steve wasn't helping things. I couldn't tell if his fingertips were creeping me out, making my nerve endings tingle, or giving me some very fine pleasure indeed.

"Let's just hope that it doesn't come to that."

Concerning the fingertips, I chose the latter. I took Steve's hand and kissed his fingers. "I don't know how long it will be before Nichols's committee meets." I shrugged. "Of course, I guess it doesn't matter. There's not much hope they'll give me a scholarship anyway."

"Would you get out of this blue funk, bro? You've still got a chance here." Steve's desperate move to make me happy was working.

"Damn," I said. "Why didn't I ask him when they meet? Maybe I'll call him." I jerked my cell from my pocket and flipped it open. As I started to punch in the number, a thought stopped me: "No, I don't want to bother him. Nobody likes a nuisance."

I put my phone back in my pocket. Lord, I was screwed up.

"Would you quit obsessing here?" Steve said. "Just give the man some time to work his magic. I'm sure he'll get back to you soon. You gave him your number, right?"

Again with the magic fingertips.

Shivers.

"Yeah, I gave it to him."

"So—he'll call you. No prob."

"Yeah, yeah," I was trying to reassure myself that all would be okay. "I'll just keep my phone on. He has my number," I said again, branding the comforting thought into my brain. "If he calls during school, I'll just have to talk my way out of detention." I was feeling better about everything, thanks to Steve, so I guess that's when I remembered: "And speaking of numbers, I need to give you my cell...."

I heard the rattle of the front door and looked toward the lobby. Standing at the top of the aisle was Her Honor, Board President Tina Silver, she of the wrinkled skin and golden straw hair.

"Who's here?" she called into the shadows.

"It's me... Nick," I yelled. I figured Steve would echo with his name, but she kept on before he could say anything.

"Why are you here today?" She always sounded annoyed, like the earth was supposed to check in with her before it revolved.

I had to make up something fast. I knew the theater was dark—that, in itself, might seem suspicious—but if she could see me, she could see Steve too. There was no telling what scene might be playing in her head. I doubt that she would approve of *her* theater being a meeting place for horny teenagers.

So I told her, "Just checking everything out for dress rehearsal tonight, Tina."

"That's what I like about you, Nick. You go the extra mile," she said, in her officious way. "I checked with Zach this morning, and he said everything was fine. But it doesn't hurt to double-check, does it?"

"No, ma'am," I said.

She turned and left, I guess to go to the office.

I turned back in my seat.

Steve was gone. I couldn't believe that guy. He flitted in and out of there like a phantom. Maybe I should call him the Phantom of the Laughton.

CHAPTER 7

OPENING NIGHT—the most exciting night in theater. Adrenaline pumping; love flowing. And flowers everywhere... that's a big tradition—to bring flowers for the actresses. And gifts—everyone gives gifts. They call them *good show* gifts. And don't ever say *good luck*. Good luck is bad luck. In the theater, we say *break a leg*.

Theater people are very superstitious. We read this Shakespeare play this year in senior English called *Macbeth*. Well, don't *ever* say that name backstage. In the dressing room, it's called *the Scottish Play*. I said *Macbeth* once before I knew not to, and you would have thought the roof would fall in from all the shouts of "no, no, no." They made me turn around three times counterclockwise, then spit over my left shoulder. Like I said, theater people are very superstitious.

I was in the booth, doing my preshow checklist. I didn't know where Steve was. He'd been there a few minutes before, but in his *way*, he'd vanished. I'd learned to expect that from him. And I'd also decided it had nothing to do with me. That's just the way he was.

And, besides... I had a ton of things to do before the show. I couldn't worry about him.

I heard the door to the booth open. My heart skipped a beat as I smiled and swung around, "St—"

I stopped midword. I guess my expression changed.

"What?" Zach said. "You're not happy to see me, son?"

I quickly tried to mask my disappointment. "No, *Daddy*." I punched the word, emphasizing our continual joke about how he calls me *son* all the time. "I just wasn't expecting you."

"Who were you expecting?"

I gulped. "No one. You just startled me."

Zach gave me strange look, but he quickly recovered. "Did you do the checklist yet? How about the headset? Is it working? Do we need new batteries? Is it too hot in here?"

For a usually calm and easygoing guy, Zach was a wreck on opening night.

It was then I noticed that someone else hovered in the doorway behind Zach.

Not just any someone. This was a particularly gorgeous someone. Instinctively, I ripped off my glasses.

The guy must have known the crazy, uptight Zach because he just waited silently in the background.

"Relax, dude." I made a *stop* sign with the palm of my hand (and smiled inside because I'd used Steve's *dude*.) "Everything's A-OK."

Then I looked at Zach's companion. "Aren't you going to introduce me?"

Zach looked confused.

I looked at the guy with him, then back at Zach.

He bopped himself in the forehead. "Oh yeah!" Zach jerked the guy into the room. He could have been pissed at being so manhandled, but he looked totally amused.

"I'm surprised you could see him, son." I could have kicked him for that comment, but I still kept my glasses off in the face of this lovely specimen of male gender. "Nick Fortunati, this is my nephew Wash Vitek. I thought you two had met at some time or other."

Zach looked like he was lying, but I didn't push it.

"Hey, man. How's it going?" I held out my fist, and we did a classic guy-thing fist bump.

"Great. And don't mind Uncle Zach. He gets this way sometimes."

So, he did totally understand. Good looks and sensitive—great combo.

"Yeah, I know. Every opening night," I quipped.

"If you think this is bad, you should see him at family stuff. Weddings, christenings—he falls apart."

We both laughed at Zach's expense.

"Go ahead," Zach said. "Make fun of the old man." He turned to Wash. "You want to sit downstairs, or do you want to stay here with Nick and learn something?" He looked at me. "It's all right if he stays in the booth, isn't it?"

Like I had a choice after he'd already proposed the idea. But I didn't mind. I was ready to kick back before the show. This guy wouldn't be a problem. Of course, once the show started, I'd be busy, but you have a pretty great view of the action from the booth, so that would keep him entertained.

"Sure, no prob," I said.

After a resounding "Break a leg," Zach left, and Wash and I sat at the control board.

"Wash? That's different," I said, fiddling with the knobs on the board, thanking Dionysius that I could see up close pretty good.

"Family name. My mother's maiden name was Washington, so I became Washington Lee Vitek… Wash, for short. You in school?"

"Dulles. You?"

"Senior at Pius."

"Pius, huh? I know someone who graduated there last year. Steve Stripling."

Wash shook his head. "Don't know him. But I just transferred in this year. We used to live in Richmond."

"Oh. So that's why Zach's never brought you around before."

"You didn't buy that 'I thought you two had met' stuff, either, huh? I think that was my Uncle Zach's not-so-subtle attempt to throw us together."

"Two minutes to curtain," I heard in the headset.

I stared out at the blurry stage. I could avoid the inevitable no longer. I slipped my glasses back on, reluctantly.

"Nice glasses," Wash said.

I looked at him, and he smiled. Strange comment. My glasses were functional, but I didn't think I'd label them "nice."

"They get the job done," I said. How could I be so lame? I started to say something else—to redeem myself from that last remark—but I heard the stage manager's voice in the headset: "And we're up."

"We're starting," I said. "I'll be busy until intermission, Wash." Then I quickly added, "Glad you're here, though." I turned to concentrate on the show, feeling like a fool. *I'm King Lame-o tonight.*

Wash sat quietly, not bothering me through the entire first act.

At intermission, Zach delivered two Cokes. We stood outside the booth to drink them. Drinks are *verboten* in the booth.

I found out that Wash was on the debate team at Pius, that he'd run for student council president—and lost—and that he didn't have a girlfriend. When I heard the two-minute warning in my headset, we slipped back in the booth.

As I sat down, I realized we had talked about Wash the whole time. He'd kept trying to ask me questions, but I'd kept shooting him down with more questions about him. I'm a smart guy. I know exactly why I do things like that. I know I think I don't measure up, that no one wants to hear about me and my life. That they only ask questions to be polite. That they don't really care about loser me. So I'd deflected his interrogation with questions about him. That served two purposes: he didn't find out that I was a nothing guy, and I got to explore him entirely. Or as entirely as a fifteen-minute intermission allowed.

I didn't know why I was so fascinated by the guy.

Act Two ended; the curtain came down. Everything had gone perfectly. The special effect had done its job; that ghost had just wafted to heaven, and the audience had gasped, as we'd hoped. The applause was deafening.

"Great show," Wash said as I hung the headphones on the hook. He had an incredibly beautiful smile.

We stood.

"Yeah, it went well," I said. *Perfect, bozo. Just stare. After all, you can't think of anything to say to this gorgeous hunk standing next to you. Loser.*

Eternity. Just staring. Then Wash said, "Well, thanks for letting me sit with you, guy. It was great meeting you." He turned to leave.

I had to do something. It was time to man up. To grow that pair I so desperately needed.

I grabbed his arm, hoping my sweaty palm wouldn't soak his shirtsleeve.

"What? You're not going to the party?"

There. I'd said it. I guess. Or had I just thought it? I was so confused.

"Party?" Wash asked.

There is always a big bash on opening night. It usually is at a cast member's house, but this production had been underwritten by one of the bigwig patrons. He was throwing the party at the Criterion Club, a swanky joint that usually only the snoots get to go to.

I'd figured that Steve and I would go together. I'd meant to ask him about it the day before, but Tina's unexpected arrival had quashed that. After my encounter with *Madam President*, I hadn't seen Steve again. And he hadn't stuck around earlier that night for me to ask him anything.

Confession time: as much I liked Steve, I was kinda glad that he hadn't stuck around. Now—since I'd made the bold move—I had a chance to take Wash with me.

"Is that an invitation?" Wash broke out a big smile.

Wow. He's glad I asked. And was I glad that my gonads were considerably larger, finally.

"Consider yourself officially invited." With the confidence that only bigger balls can provide, I shot him a smile as warm as I had gotten. This was monumental. Was this going to be a date? If so, had I just asked a guy out? I guess I had. A date. I was going on a date. My first. With a guy.

So I took Wash as my date. Before we made it there, I'd crawled back in my closet. I'd convinced myself it wasn't really a date. It was dark in that closet, but it felt safe somehow. Even though I did feel a definite shrinkage in the *you know* area.

No, Wash was just hanging with me at the party, just like he had done all night. No strings attached. My God, he didn't act gay, anyway. I know, I know—there's no such thing as "acting gay" unless you count the campy, nelly queens. You know, the ones who swish around, calling everyone *girl* and twirling filmy scarves and such. Don't get me wrong—if they're happy, then I say more power to them. At least they're out in the open about who they are. Says the big old homo in the dark, dark box.

No, I was reasonably certain that Wash, even if I wanted his beautiful body, was not available to those of my persuasion. I was so sure that I refused to let myself even hope.

But the party was fantastic. There was a huge buffet spread—it was a Mexican fiesta: shrimp, chicken, and beef fajitas; guacamole, sour cream, cheese—both *chili con queso* and shredded, *pico de gallo*, *frijoles*, rice, warm flour tortillas, corn chips. The chef at this club really knew his Mexican food. And there was a huge celebration cake, decorated with the poster of the show, sprayed on with edible paint. Wow. I figured this was the chef's only concession to north-of-the-border food, but when the cake was cut, it proved to be *tres leches*.

It's a wonder I don't weigh a ton, because I really like to eat. Wash matched me taco for taco, though, so I didn't feel bad.

And there was an open bar. The bartenders were checking IDs but not real thoroughly. I noticed that people who looked younger than me were drinking. I probably could have had my fill of anything I wanted.

But I don't drink. I know—I sound like a nerd, but I don't believe in drinking and driving, and since I was driving, there was no way I was going to risk anything.

It was kinda funny, what happened right after we got there. Wash pointed to the bar and asked if I wanted a drink. I told him I didn't drink but that he was welcome to it. Well, his reply was that he didn't drink either, that he was just trying to be sociable. We both laughed at that. Who would have thought there'd be two teenage boys in the world who didn't like alcohol—or at least would admit it?

But even without strong spirits, Wash and I had a great time. He was so funny. He made me laugh, and that's something I don't do enough of.

I did keep scanning the room for Steve, but he never showed. Here I had the perfect setup to make him a little jealous, and the guy wasn't there. Pissed me off. I'd never been in this position before. Two guys on the string. Granted, I didn't know if Wash was gay, and Steve was obviously on a very loose string, but a man could hope, couldn't he? Gay or not, Wash could make anybody jealous. And Steve deserved it after standing me up.

It sounds like I was fuming about it all, or that I was so mad at Steve that I was ready to deck him if I saw him. But that's not true.

Truth be told, Wash was, for the most part, keeping me delightfully distracted.

Wash was in the middle of this story about a thing that happened in his history class, when Zach strode up. He had a newspaper in his hand.

"You guys having fun?" he asked.

"Sure are, Uncle Zach," Wash answered.

"I thought you two would hit it off," he said, winking.

Wink? Why the wink? Come on, Zach. Was this a setup? And if so, then do you know that I'm gay? And if you know, why doesn't my dad know? I quickly deleted that last thought because I was having fun, and *Dad/me gay* thoughts do not add up to fun.

Suddenly, it dawned on me why Zach had the newspaper. "Is that the Laughton story? I saw it being passed around backstage, but I never got to read it. They were hogging the copies, and I needed to get to the booth. Let me see. Let me see."

"Here." He handed me the paper. "Quit begging like a little puppy."

I looked down at the page he had turned back.

Under the headline "Historic Theater Still Going Strong," there was a half-page story. Included with the story were three pics. The last one, I recognized: it was a shot of our current show they had snapped last week. The first picture was of the front of the Laughton, all lit up with floodlights. The caption read, "The gala premiere night of the theater—1939."

The middle one was labeled *1989*. It was of a stripper in midstrip. The shot was taken from backstage. Across the way, on the other side of the wings, a few guys stood watching the dancer. The guys were in shadows, lit by the spill of the stage lights. But something was strange.

I held the paper closer, peering at the men in the shot. With a flash of recognition, a weird feeling flooded me.

One of the men standing in the shot was not a man at all. He was a young guy, dressed all in black.

And he was a dead ringer for Steve.

CHAPTER 8

IT WAS almost impossible to get through the rest of the party. I tried not to show that there was anything strange in the news I'd seen.

I guess I did an okay job concealing everything, because Wash grabbed the paper from me and read the story. Then he handed it back to Zach.

"No," Zach said, tossing me the paper, "this is for Nick's scrapbook. I got plenty more copies." Then he left.

The rest of the night, Wash continued trying to entertain me. I smiled and laughed, but I really didn't hear a word he was saying.

About midnight, I looked at my watch and mumbled about having to get home. Wash walked me to my car and said good night. He also said, "Maybe we can hook up again sometime," but I was so filled with Steve thoughts that I think I ignored him or just offered a feeble "yeah."

My mind raced all the way home and half the night. How in the holy hell could Steve be in a picture taken over twenty years ago? I asked myself that over and over again. It began to be a mantra rather than a real question that I wanted to know the answer to. It was weird. I wanted to know the answer, but then again, the possibilities were so surreal that I didn't want to know. I was a mess. Nothing was going to solve the problem anytime soon. I was just losing sleep over a conundrum (SAT vocabulary word—look it up.)

Luckily, logic kicked in, or I would have been awake the whole night. That had to be a picture of Steve's dad, or an uncle, or second cousin twice removed, for all I knew. I only knew that there was no way it could be Steve in that picture.

But why hadn't Steve ever mentioned this guy before? He'd never said anything about family working at the strip joint.

Maybe, I decided, he didn't know.

But whatever, I knew I had to show that pic to Steve.

And I had to get some sleep.

I would talk to Steve at Saturday night's show.

But in typical Steve fashion, he was not there. This was getting to be a pain. Yeah, I got it that he wouldn't show if there was a crowd, but come on, we were getting to be a twosome and he needed to get over this shy act.

So I was faced with another night before I could get into the theater when no one else would be around.

Mom insists on church Sunday mornings, but I could see Steve in the afternoon. That is, if—and given the fact that Steve had not shown his face after the show the night before—he was at the Laughton that afternoon. Why do I have a cell phone if I'm not going to give out my number and get others'? Loser, loser, loser.

With the show up and running, and no matinee, Zach had asked me to go to the theater and clean up the storage room—and, of course, replace the lightbulb.

So, after church, I grabbed a sandwich and pointed my wheels toward the Laughton.

My plan was a simple one: show Steve his twin in the paper and give Steve hell for not being there last night. I was pretty whipped up over that when I thought of Wash, and then I felt guilty. Who was I to demand explanations?

First Steve was all I could think about, and then I met Wash. We had a fantastic time at the party, and I felt like I was in love all over again. If I was so head over heels with Steve, then I should have forgotten Wash by then, don't you think?

So now you see where my mind was when the gargoyles greeted me that Sunday. And just after their hiss came a kiss—a big, demanding one. Steve came from behind, grabbed me, swung me around, planted one on me, and just like that—those incredibly green eyes knocked any thoughts of Wash or that picture clean out of my mind. Steve was some good kisser.

Things got heavy fast. I was beginning to think that Steve had some mystical power over me. One kiss, and I melted. Of course, that *one* kiss was always an intoxicating one.

I could have succumbed, but no: reason took over. I had a job to do. I take commitments seriously, and being Zach's assistant is the strongest commitment I have. I'm almost bound to him. A covenant.

And besides, other crew heads sometimes showed up on the Sunday after opening. That would be just great—someone catching me and Steve going at it there right at center stage. *Zach would be so proud of his son.*

So I pulled away, reluctant and confused. After all, I may be a loser and a loner, but I'm a horny loser and loner. There was no way I *wanted* to end this; I just knew I *had* to.

I grabbed Steve by the arm. "Enough, lover boy. We've got work to do." I pulled him to the storeroom, where, of course, the light was out.

Standing in the dark, Steve lunged for me again. He enveloped me, and I felt his hot breath closing in. I wanted to succumb. Truth to tell, I was not simply horny; I was feeling a strong connection, feeling cared for, nurtured, loved. But I couldn't let Zach down. No distractions. At least until my work was done.

"Stop it, Steve." I pushed him away. "I want this as much as you do, but I promised Zach I'd work. And I can't do that with you pawing me."

"Pawing? Is that what you think this is? Just groping in the dark?" I heard the hurt in his voice.

"Sorry, guy. Bad choice of words. If I could, I'd take you to bed and do this all day long. But I promised Zach. I can't be distracted, no matter how delicious the distraction is. And your lips are delicious." I reached out and brushed my hand against his cheek, which I could barely make out from the outside light spilling in the doorway. "Okay?"

"Okay. What do we need to do?"

"First thing first. We need to shed some light on this mess." We keep the spare lightbulbs on a shelf near the door so we can easily see them as we come in. I grabbed one.

Hoping I'd appeased Steve with that *take you to bed* crack, I decided it was time to probe. I wanted to know why he'd deserted me opening night.

"You missed an awesome party last night. Where were you?" I started out slow, friendly. Maybe if I didn't sound confrontational, he'd be more open to answering honestly. So I played it cool as I changed the lightbulb. "I was kinda hoping on sharing it with my boyfriend, ya know."

"I'm not much for crowds." He took the sleeve that the bulb had been in and turned to toss it in the garbage. "Besides, I noticed you weren't exactly lonely. I saw you and your new conquest in the booth last night."

That was a pissy thing to say. Then again, I had hoped to make him jealous. I guess it worked.

Well, he could be as pissy as he wanted. If he couldn't show his face to me, if he was lurking around, spying on me, well, then, I didn't owe him any explanations.

"You, no doubt, are talking about Wash?" I fed his anger. Two could play.

"Is that his name? I'm afraid," he spat, "we weren't introduced."

He stared at me, piercing me with those emeralds. I tossed the ball right back into his court.

"If you'd stick around sometime, you might meet more people. You're always disappearing, dude."

I started moving the scoops around, arranging them on the floor so they were no longer in the way. And I was giving him time to process. We'd never progress together if he didn't realize that relationships were a two-way street.

"I hear you." I could still hear cold, steel anger. "Spill it. I noticed that guy's hot; I would guess you noticed too." Venom was in his voice.

I was no longer playing this game. "Well, I'm not dead." I tossed what I hoped was the winning volley over my shoulder.

I grabbed a broom and began sweeping.

Steve just stood there. I guess he was waiting for more of an answer. I almost gave him what he wanted, but at the last minute, thankfully, I decided to try to salvage this. It was time I said the words.

"But I also am in love—with you, guy." There. I said 'em. I couldn't take it back, even if I wanted to. "Wash is gorgeous, but he's not you."

I'd dodged a bullet. That was all it took. Steve smiled.

"So, tell me about the party," he said, grabbing the dustpan.

As we scooped up the pile I'd made, I told him all about the people there and the food. I was glad to be off the Wash topic and onto something inane like the party. But in the middle of reciting the menu, I remembered. All the tension over Steve's desertion and Wash had completely blocked me. The reason for my sleepless nights had slipped my mind entirely.

I pulled the newspaper clipping out of my back pocket.

"This is going to blow you away, man," I said as I unfolded the clipping. "Did you see this in yesterday's *Trib*?" I handed over the clipping.

He stared at the paper for what seemed like a full minute or two. Apparently he hadn't seen it the day before.

Then a sigh broke his silence. "Oh my God."

"You noticed too, huh? Is that guy a dead ringer for you or what? Who is he? You know him? Your uncle? Your cousin?"

I expected an immediate answer. It had to be a relative. It was the only explanation.

But Steve kept staring at the picture. I was about to ask him again who it was when he gave me his answer.

"It's me."

He said it so matter-of-factly, without emotion. What was I supposed to think? Steve had come face-to-face with a ghost from his past. Maybe he didn't know who the guy was. Maybe he was in shock that a total stranger could look so much like him.

"Yeah, I know... it really could be." I pointed at the pic. "The same hair, the same build, even the same clothes. Weird, huh?"

Steve stared at me, a blank stare. I couldn't read anything into that look. I've heard of people going into shock, but not from seeing a news clipping.

Then, quietly, he said "It's me" again.

"Oh yeah—" I nodded and turned to pick up a bunch of gel holders that had fallen to the floor of the storeroom. "—1989... the guy in the picture must be eighteen or nineteen. That would make you, what? Late thirties? Early forties? Sure, *old man*."

Steve grabbed me and swung me around. "I'm telling you, Nick, the guy in this picture is me. Can't you see it? Or do you need new specs?"

"But that's impossible. You're my age—or almost. That can't be you in this picture." Was he losing it?

He put both his hands on my shoulders and looked me straight in the eyes. "Do you think I'd lie to you?"

That bothered me. He didn't seem to be in shock anymore. He looked to me like he was in total control, serious.

It threw me. What was he saying to me?

"I swear that the guy in this picture is me, Stephen Stripling."

His eyes were clear, resolute. His voice, steady.

He scared me a little. What if he freaked on me? He looked totally rational, but he wasn't acting rational.

For the first time in my life, I knew what real fear was.

I'd left my phone in my car, so the best I could do was inch my way out to the lobby, just in case. I could use the phone in the box office if I needed to call in reinforcements. I'd seen TV shows where they have to call in the guys in the white jackets, but I never thought that was something I would have to do.

Then that voice you read about kicked in: that still, small voice. What was I thinking? This was a guy I loved. I hadn't known him long, but I was certain he wouldn't hurt me. I simply had to play along, just reason with him.

"Okay, it's you. Why haven't you aged all these years?" I made my voice sound light, conversational. I freed the tension in my body. I willed myself to act casual. "Walk with me. I need to call my mom," I lied.

I edged my way past him and out of the little room. Slowly, I made my way toward the lobby, chattering inane things. *Mom had a headache when we left church. We'd stopped at a drugstore for Tylenol. Only rest helps her when she's like this. I need to call and check on her.* Anything to keep talking and to get him—and me—near a telephone.

He followed me.

"My mom was one of the dancers."

I guess all that talk about my mother triggered his remark.

"Really? Tell me about her," I said, as I pushed the lobby door open.

"Well, at least, she used to be." Steve kept talking as we made it into the lobby. The flood of light calmed my nerves. And Steve didn't seem so scary anymore.

"She finally ended up selling tickets. I did all sorts of odd jobs here. I helped her in the box office, I set lights, I even cleaned the dressing rooms."

"But that's not possible, Steve." He'd never acted crazy before, and his matter-of-factness spoke volumes. He gave the appearance of being perfectly sane, but this just wasn't making sense. "What are you? A time traveler? You get in your time machine and zap yourself to the Laughton to see me?" I tried to keep my voice even, light. I refused to push him over the edge. For my sake *and* his.

I pulled him over to a bench and sat him down. Then I joined him.

"Don't you remember the first time we met?" he continued. "I told you then that I'm here all the time."

"So am I," I countered. "What does that prove?"

"No, Nick, you only come here for a few hours at a time." He gestured around him. "I never leave this place."

"Oh, right." That last was too, too flip. I couldn't have him thinking I was humoring him, although that's probably what I was doing. I put my arm on his. "You never eat, you never shower, you never see your family." I said it calmly, pointedly, hoping to gently jolt him back to reality.

"My family is dead. Or at least, my mom is." He looked down at his feet. "I told you before that I never had a dad."

What was going on here? Steve had never, ever given me reason to question him. True, I didn't know a whole lot about him, but he'd always seemed rational, a normal guy just like me. He had a great sense of humor, and he was very caring. He'd helped me work through some problems. And, I couldn't forget, he was a great kisser.

I just couldn't make myself believe that I had anything to fear from Steve, nor did he seem to be lying. So that only left one conclusion. And if I accepted that, then I might be as crazy as I had thought he was. But I couldn't let him sit there looking so lost.

I tugged at his sleeve. He fell into my arms. As we hugged, I said, "I'm sorry I didn't believe you, Steve. I really am."

The moment I said that, I realized how stupid it sounded. Nothing he'd said could be true. But he needed me, and when someone needs you, you say what they want to hear.

I let him sob, giving him time to release the demon inside him. He was lying, but it had to be to cover something that was so totally heinous that he couldn't tell me about it.

As his tears started to subside, I pulled away gently, held his cheeks in my hands, and looked him in the eyes. I had to try again.

"You can't possibly live in a cold, dark theater, Steve."

"Think about it, Nick." His voice caught. He was going to cry again. But he caught himself. "Have we ever left here together?" He stood, walked two steps, his back to me.

"No, but so what?"

"And these clothes I'm wearing." He turned, gesturing to his all-black threads.

"Yeah, I admit you have unusual taste in clothes, but what does that prove?"

"What do the people backstage wear for every show, Nick? Huh? What?"

"They're all in black so that if they're caught on stage during a scene change, it's less noticeab—" It hit me like a ton of bricks. And I didn't like what I was hearing.

I couldn't see it, but I felt it—the look on my face. Confusion. Horror. Disbelief. Total and utter brain chaos.

"Exactly." He measured his words, no doubt handling me with the kid gloves I had recently handled him with. "I'm dressed in the clothes I wore when I worked. And they're the same clothes each time you see me, aren't they, Nick?"

I didn't have an answer for him. My mind was speeding, grasping for reality.

"You're joking, aren't you, Steve?" But he wasn't smiling. I looked around, searching for an answer to all this.

It was his turn to sit next to me to offer support.

"I just can't believe, Steve, that you live in this theater."

I can't for the life of me understand why I did it, but I stood, grabbed him, and pulled him back into the auditorium. I knew I found my comfort, my reality, in this old theater, and the lobby just wasn't this theater to me. Too generic. But here, in the dark space, life was real.

I took Steve's arm and pointed it. "The only residents of this old place are the gargoyles and the phantoms of past shows."

"Maybe that's what I am." I followed his eyes as they stared out at the walls where the gargoyles, in all their hideous Technicolor glory, kept watch.

"A gargoyle?" I laughed. Unconvincingly, but a laugh none the same. An attempt to deflect what was going on. This was heavy. Too heavy for me to process.

"You're too hot to be a gargoyle, Steve." A feeble attempt at humor. True statement, but I was hoping to snap him back. To snap me back. Because I was ready to plunge off Steve's cliff.

He took a step away from me.

"Then I guess—" He sighed. "—I'm a phantom."

"A *phantom*? You mean a ghost?" I almost doubled over in laughter at that. Tension can do strange things. Like, make you laugh when nothing's funny. "A real, live ghost?"

"No, Nick, I mean a real, *dead* ghost."

CHAPTER 9

THE WAY he said it stopped me in my tracks. No more laughter, nervous or otherwise. This guy was serious.

"Come on, guy, I'm not buying that," I reasoned, still trying to convince him—no, me—that this was a crazy idea.

"Think about it." He took a couple of steps toward the front of the stage. "Have you ever seen me outside of this place?"

I didn't respond. I wasn't playing into this, but I couldn't figure a way out, either.

Suddenly, Steve turned to me.

"Have you ever seen me, like, talk to anyone but you?" he blurted out, a look in his eyes that said *you've got to believe me.*

I licked my suddenly dry lips.

"Has anyone you've told about me said that they know who you're talking about?" He stepped toward me.

"I've only mentioned you to Zach. And he hasn't been here that long," I stammered, like I was failing to compute. It flashed in my mind that I'd also mentioned him to Wash, but bringing up Wash would only complicate this more. And this idea was maddening. I didn't need further complications. I refused to believe the lame-ass story he was dishing out. But Steve was bent on convincing me. And he was doing a pretty good job, despite my clinging to what I thought was reality.

He took two more steps in my direction. "So, maybe Zach hasn't been here that long, but if I've done as much around here as I claim, don't you think he would have heard about me?"

I shuddered. I needed to run from there—run as far away as I could. This was asinine. But I just stood there. Why?

He—was—making—sense.

And that scared me. Abject terror. I was losing my mind. I was in an empty theater in a bad neighborhood with a loony. And believing him.

He was right on me, holding my chin, his eyes piercing me. "Nick, I've been stuck here for the last twenty years or so. I lost count a long time ago. At first, I didn't know what was happening. Then I figured it out."

I couldn't move. "Figured what out?" I mumbled.

"I'm trapped here for a reason. I don't know why, but I do know I can't leave."

No, no, no, no, no, no, no. I am not a fool. And he wasn't going to make me one.

I broke away and bounded past him up the aisle.

About halfway up, something turned me around.

"Okay… so say I believe you. Why would you be trapped? I go to church. I know all about heaven and stuff. If you're dead, you should have gone to heaven—or, God forbid, hell—a long time ago. Why would you be doomed to spend eternity in a drafty old theater?"

"I've thought about that. Believe me, I've had plenty of time to think around here. But I can't come up with a reason."

I was insane. Total madness. You'd expect to be drooling when you're insane, but there I was, totally dry mouthed, accepting his every word.

He was making sense about this ghost thing.

I found myself walking back up the aisle toward Steve.

"The last thing I remember was talking to my mom's best friend." He came toward me, meeting me as he talked. "And I don't recall what we talked about. Sometime after that, something happened that I don't want to remember."

"What? Why wouldn't you want to remember the last moments of your life?" I was getting into this and didn't hear how idiotic I must have sounded.

"I think I was offed... killed. I don't know why. I don't know when. But something must have happened that I've blocked out. Heavy, huh?"

"Incredible. So you've been shacked up here for over twenty years? And you've never put forth this theory to anyone before me?" This was too, too mind-boggling. I took a breath—a clean, long breath.

I could not, would not, should not believe what I was believing. I guess sometimes things just don't make sense.

"I've never been able to talk to anyone before you, Nick. I've been so lonely. But then I watched you. I saw how lonely you were. There was something about you. I could tell we were alike, you and I, that it would be safe for me to talk to you. It's funny—I tried to show myself a couple of other times, but I couldn't do it. I guess something just told me that you were the one. I was trapped, and you freed me."

Steve was really getting into his story, and I was starting to feel uneasy again. I had one chance to wipe this from my mind. I could walk away. And that's what I did.

I walked past him and up the steps. I was leaving, leaving this place and this lunatic. "Tell this to someone who believes you."

I was halfway to the door, far away from where we'd been standing, and yet I felt him right behind me. So much for walking away.

"You've got to believe me, Nick. This isn't bunk. I'm coming clean here because, you see, I think you were sent to me. Sent to solve the puzzle."

He turned me around, leaned in, and kissed me.

A quiver rippled through me. That kiss somehow made me accept everything he said. I can't explain it. It was as if that single kiss was filled with every answer to every question I'd ever asked myself about Steve. That kiss told me how very much he loved me, how trapped he felt, how much he needed me. If Steve needed his murder solved, then I was going to be the man to do it.

"So, where do I start?" I asked.

CHAPTER 10

DAMN. ONCE I left the theater, the doubts came back in full force. I'd always thought I was a levelheaded guy, but I was starting to think my elevator wasn't going to the top floor.

I'd swallowed Steve's story… my boyfriend's a ghost. Oh yeah… *and* he was murdered. Give me a break. But, then again, this was coming from my boyfriend, of all people. Who can you believe if not your boyfriend?

So, say I believed him, then what? If he was killed, why? Did he know something, do something, that someone didn't like? Maybe he deserved it. Maybe he was into some evil crap that had to be stopped. I was sounding like Batman did him in.

But that did give me something to wrap my mind around. My boyfriend may have been a bad, bad dude.

Oh great—I finally found a boyfriend, and he might be a gangster or worse. Could my life get any more complicated?

I hit the button on the armrest, and my window slid down. Cool, calming air flooded in.

It didn't help much. I deserved to be addled over these latest developments—and I was. But I was also obsessed with the fact that I, Nick Fortunati, had a boyfriend, and I couldn't stop saying the word over and over in my mind.

And, adding to everything, when I got home, Dad was bat-shit crazy. He was grinning from one considerably big ear to the other. Thank God I got my ears from my mother.

He pounced on me as soon as I got in the door, laughing and spouting gibberish. Something like "Here's my boy" and crap like that. The man was actually dancing a jig around me. I didn't know where Mom was, but if she'd been there, I'd have her say "Leave the boy alone."

"Why are you so happy?"

He stopped dancing long enough to tell me that his boss had called. The committee had met that afternoon. I was one of the finalists for the scholarship.

My world collapsed.

I was going to spend my life in bio-lab hell. So much for that pair I grew. I couldn't say a word to Dad. Could it get any worse?

Oh yeah, it could. I forgot. My boyfriend was a ghost.

I dragged myself to school the next morning, having not slept at all—zip—*nada*. Tell me you could sleep with all that hanging over your head.

First thing in civics, Apley pulled out a test. Crap. I'd forgotten. Now, that just doesn't happen to me. I absolutely do not forget about tests. I might forget other things, but school stuff is sacred to me.

You see, when I was in first grade, my dad said he'd give me a dollar for a straight-A report card. Well, after I earned that first dollar, I got addicted. I know—what a dork. A dollar won't buy anything. But, I don't know, I just get this rush every six weeks when Dad hands over that dollar.

So now, to add to the my-boyfriend's-a-ghost-and-I'm-a-lab-geek thing, I had to fake my way through a civics test, no less. Thank God I usually paid attention in class. I didn't ace the test, but at least I passed it, and it didn't totally crash my grade.

And the day only went downhill from there. In English, we had to discuss a chapter of *Wuthering Heights*, which I hadn't read, of course. Calculus found us learning a new theorem that I couldn't grasp because my mind was elsewhere.

And I even tanked in gym, where I usually excel. You see, my PE teacher's the wrestling coach. He's taught us a lot of great moves. He even asked me once to join the team, but wrestling's not my thing, you know? Well, that day he didn't beg me to join his team, that's for sure. Since I hadn't had any sleep the night before, I sucked.

By the time the day was over, I was ready to crash. I headed to Koffee Kart for a latte and some free Wi-Fi. But even my favorite website couldn't improve my mood. No, not even Gay Met Youth could do it for me. It just put me in a fouler mood than ever. On top of all my problems, I realized I was a total loser because I was stuck in a deep, dark closet and was never getting out.

And that made me think of Steve. If he was a ghost—I still wasn't totally convinced—I had to find out for myself. And the first person to talk to was that reporter, the one who'd written the article that started all this.

I googled the *Tribune*, got the number, pulled out my cell, and punched.

"You've reached the offices of the *Tribune*. If you know your...."

You know the drill. I waited until that annoying voice finished, punched in the first three letters of the reporter's last name (since I didn't know his extension) and eventually got—you guessed it—his voice mail.

"Wunnenberg here. I'm either away from my desk or taking another call. Leave your name and...."

Deep breath.... I left my name and number and hoped he would return the call.

I ordered another latte and sat back down. As I was halfway through chapter twelve of *Wuthering*, my phone rang.

"Mr. Fortunati? Wunnenberg. You wanted something?"

"Thanks, Mr. Wunnenberg. And it's Nick, please." If I charmed him, it could only help, so I greased every word with cinnamon butter. Then I fed him the story I had concocted. "I have a teacher who's a real hard-ass about local history. We have to do a project. Well, I saw your article on the Laughton and figured that you'd already done half of my work for me." I laughed, trying to sound even more conversational.

"And you want my research, right?" he said. Did I detect annoyance in his voice?

"Not exactly." I didn't want to lose him. I added some honey to the cinnamon butter. "I found the early stuff about the Laughton at the public library. They have tons of stuff, as *you*, of course, know."

"Yeah. So what can I do for you?"

"Well, the middle stuff—the strip joint stuff—is where I hit a dead end. Would you be willing to share your source with me?" I had my voice dripping with so much kindness that I must have sounded like a honey-drippin', li'l ol' Southern belle. I'd seen all the headlines about reporters not revealing sources, but I hoped since this wasn't exactly a corruption-at-City-Hall-type story, he would tell me something.

But nothing comes easy, does it?

"Nick, what say we meet somewhere? I just met my deadline, so I was heading out for some coffee."

Well, maybe things do come easy.

"Great. I'm at KK right now—the one at the corner of Fifth and Fillmore," I said.

"That's not far from here," Wunnenberg said. "I could be there in fifteen. Sound okay? I'm always happy to help a budding journalist."

"I'll sit tight, then. Thanks, Mr. Wunnenberg."

I nursed my latte, thoughts flashing like neon lights in my brain, trying to think of every angle I could work with him. I got so wrapped up in my scheming that I almost jumped when I heard my name.

My eyes jerked up to see a tall guy about Dad's age hovering above me.

"Nick?" he repeated.

I leapt up and grabbed his hand, shaking it. "Sorry. I was daydreaming, I guess. Mr. Wunnenberg?"

"Call me Hal."

"Hal it is." I liked that he was so friendly, plus my quest might be easier won if we were on a first-name basis.

"I'm going to grab some coffee," he said. "Can I get you anything?"

"Thanks, Hal." I read somewhere that people like it if you use their name a lot. "A dolce latte, thanks."

I sat back down to wait for him and the coffees. As I pondered my next move, I started to feel guilty about using the guy. I wasn't brought up to be a user, but then again, I also wasn't brought up to believe in ghosts.

He handed me my coffee, then sat in the chair across the table from me.

He took a long draft of his coffee, then sighed. "Ah-h-h. Beats the swill in the city room any day."

He gulped some more, then looked me straight in the eye. "Okay, Nick, tell me more about this assignment of yours."

"Well," I started, saying a silent prayer that he would buy my story, then also apologizing to God for using him that way. "I'm a senior at Dulles, and I took the local history class just to burn off a credit. Mr. Link, my teacher, assigned this project that counts for half of our grade... so much for easy credit. Well, Hal, I just have to ace this class. I'm a theater guy—I work at Streetwise Players—and after I saw your article, I knew my project should be about the Laughton."

I didn't realize how fast I was talking until I finished and Wunnenberg said, "Okay, okay—slow down, son. Have some coffee. Relax."

That wasn't what I wanted to hear. I had hoped he'd listen to my little tale of woe and immediately give up his source. I needed him to spill.

"Link, huh? He still teaching there?"

Uh-oh. My scheme just might have hit a snag.

"Linky must be about a hundred and two by now. He was ancient when I took that course."

Dionysius, he knew Mr. Link. I had to think fast. I only knew the teacher from seeing him in the halls.

"Yeah, he's an institution at Dulles," I said, trying desperately to sound like I loved and admired the man. *You can do this, Nick*, I told myself. Make like Link is your favorite teacher. And you're his favorite student. Help me, oh god of theater.

"I remember Linky's project. I was a jock. Coach said, 'Take Link's class. Easy A.' Well, Coach was full of crap. I worked my tail off on that project. I did more research for that thing than I've ever done for a story at the paper, ever."

Maybe I could use that to my advantage. "So you realize how much I could use your source's name."

"Nick, my boy, Linky turned me into a journalist."

I coughed—a big, choking *harrumph*. I wasn't expecting that. What if he still talked to Mr. Link sometimes? Shit creek time.

"If it weren't for Hewlett Link, I would have pinned my hopes on a football scholarship. And those were false hopes. I never would have admitted that to anyone before I took Linky's class. I got so into that project that I found myself thinking about it on the football field at practice. That got me thinking. If I was liking all this research so much that I couldn't concentrate on the game, then maybe I didn't need to be in the game."

I slowly sipped my latte, appraising the situation. I decided this kook was too crazy to worry about. I doubted he'd ever emerged from his own little world to talk to some old teacher he'd once had. But I also found myself wondering if I was going to be able to pry anything I needed out of him.

"I quit football to devote myself to that project. My dad almost kicked me out of the house. You see, Dad just knew I was going to get an athletic scholarship. You know how dads are. Blind as bats sometimes when it comes to their kids."

Tell me about it.

"Well, I couldn't play the game and get that project done at the same time. The season kept getting in the way. And, just between you and me, Dad was a little too hyped up on me, I think. I wasn't really a very good football player."

Get to the point, I wanted to scream.

"So...." He paused and put his cup to his lips. But he didn't drink. It was like he was in another realm.

I just sat there, totally at a loss. Was this guy going to give me what I wanted or not?

Then he kind of jerked to attention, took a big gulp of coffee, grabbed his iPhone off his belt holster, and blurted out, "Nick, this is your lucky day. I'm going to set you on that path that I discovered all those years ago." He punched a bunch of buttons on his phone. "The contact who filled me in on the stripper stuff is a hoot. She'd love talking to you."

He handed the iPhone to me. "Name's Layla Burns. That's her number. She's the dancer in the picture. And let me warn you, Nick— she doesn't like to be called a stripper. She is—or was—a dancer. And she won't let you forget that—as she talks your ear off, I might add." He laughed.

I grabbed a pencil and copied the name and number into my notebook, then handed him back the phone.

He snapped the phone back into its holster.

"Now, Nick, I don't usually give up my sources this easily, but the two of us are Linked." He laughed at his joke. "Make me proud, Nick. Ace that project, like I did. Who knows? You may be a cub reporter someday."

"Who knows?" I repeated. Then I looked at my watch. "Oh my gosh," I lied. "I've got to get to the theater." I stowed my laptop, notebook, and pencil, then finished off my coffee. "Thanks, Hal. You've been a big help." I stood and extended my hand to him.

"Anytime, Nick, anytime." He smiled as he jerked my hand up and down.

I didn't know what more, if anything, I was going to learn from this Layla, but if Steve was the guy in that picture, then maybe she'd confirm it.

And if Steve was that guy, then I was in for a rough ride.

A murdered boyfriend.

A murdered ghostly boyfriend.

CHAPTER 11

THERE WAS all sorts of sleazy, afternoon-TV-talk-show type stuff running through my mind as I drove over to Layla Burns's place. When I called her on the phone, she was all *honey* this and *sweetie* that. She sounded just like my grandmother. But the strippers on the cop shows might talk sweet on one hand while they're hard as nails on the other. So I had no idea what to expect.

Tell the truth, I was venturing out of my comfort zone. But helping Steve was worth it. If visiting some retired hoochie dancer's shabby home was the price I had to pay, then so be it.

Damn, was I in for a reality check.

As I made my way through her neighborhood, I thought, *her house must be behind this subdivision. No stripper could afford anything like these.*

I did a double take when I came upon her house number. On a gate. A gigantic, elaborate gate.

I couldn't even get into her place without first talking to a guard. He came to the car and motioned for me to lower my window.

"Mr. Fortunati?" I nodded. "Mizz Burns says to pull on up. She'll meet you at the door." He was all business.

Now, the door was not just right there. I had to drive about another quarter mile, along a winding driveway, under huge shade trees. Finally, I pulled up to what only can be described as a palace: a huge, Southern plantation-style mansion. Grander than Tara, Scarlett.

And there she was—standing and waiting, just like the guard had said. I blinked. This woman could have been my own grandma. She had her hair in a bun, a pair of glasses on a cord around her neck, and a pale blue dress that could make the cover of the AARP magazine.

"Nick, honey, I see you found our little ol' place, here." Magnolias dripped from her mouth as I got out of the car and approached her.

"I'm Layla, sweetie."

She held out a hand that sported a diamond so big the sparkle flashed on the lens of my glasses and blinded me. Now, that was definitely not like my own grandma.

I took her hand and said, "Pleased to meet you, Mrs. Burns."

"Now, none of that *Mrs.* stuff. I'm just Layla, darlin'." She pulled me into a hug. "Come on into the house. We'll have us some nice cold lemonade while we visit."

I followed her into the house, and, now I'm not shitting you, there was a butler standing there in front of us, waiting for her command. That's right, a man in a penguin suit, just waiting for her orders.

"Billy, deah," she said to the butler, "could you bring our lemonade into the parlor? And bring us some of those little cakes"— she said the word like it had two syllables—"we found at the darlin' li'l bakery yesterday, would ya, honey?"

As she led me into a room off the foyer, she said, "I have such a sweet tooth, Nick. I can't, can't, can't stay away from sugary things. I have such a time maintainin' my figuah. You'll have a cake with me, won't you, baby? It will make me feel so much less guilty, Nicky."

Now, nobody but nobody calls me Nicky except my gran. So you can see how Layla had already won me over. I would do anything for her.

As she motioned me to sit on what my mom would call a *genuine antique*, my eyes caught the huge portrait over the mantel: a younger, incredibly beautiful Layla in full costume.

"I see you're admirin' my portrait," she said, sitting next to me on the couch. "My late husband had that done. It embarrassed me, his hangin' it right over the mantle theah. But he was so proud of it—*and* me. That god-awful picture has become a part of this place. Now, I wouldn't remove the thing for nothin'. Reminds me of my Sam. We met when I was dancin'. Lordy, that was a long time ago. Why, my Sam's been gone now for ten long years." This cheerful soul suddenly had a catch in her voice and a tear on her cheek. I wanted to hug her.

"What kind of work did your husband do, Layla?"

"Sam? He was a banker. Made a fortune in land speculation. I fell head over heels in love with him the first moment I laid eyes on him. He was standin' at the stage door, a big bouquet"—she pronounced it *bo-kay*, emphasis on the *bo*—"of roses in his hand."

"Cool," I said. So, I know that sounds lame, but I couldn't think of anything else to say, and I felt like I had to say something.

"Oh, Nicky, that doesn't even begin to describe it. It was rapturous!" She'd made a sudden journey to the past, and having seen that look on Gran's face before, I knew to just let her have her memories for a moment.

The butler put the lemonade tray on the table in front of us. Layla snapped back to reality.

"Thank you, Billy darlin'." She handed me a glass of lemonade and a little cake on a plate. "Now, you're here to talk about the old Palace, so why don't we go ahead on."

"Well, I know that the old theater was originally a movie theater."

"Yes," she said. "But it was on its last legs as a movie place when we moved our show in." For about fifteen minutes, she went on and on about the beginning of the Palace, as she kept calling the Laughton. Most of that stuff I already knew. Then she suddenly jumped up and ran to a glass cabinet across the room. "I've got something you'll prob'ly want to see."

She came back with an old scrapbook.

"Pictures," she squealed. She was having so much fun reliving the *old* days, as she called them. I got the impression that, despite her wealth, she was lonely. I knew that feeling well, so a sense of guilt came over me. After all, I was being deceptive with this lovely, generous lady. "I've got a passel of shots of the old place, plus I want you to see some of my friends back then."

She opened the book. "This is what it looked like when we took it over." The Laughton looked a little worse for wear. "It was a forlorn ol' barn. How very sad. It was such a showplace when it first opened." She pointed to a second pic. "And these are the dressing rooms. That's my table"—I could see her back and her reflection in the mirror—"and right next to me, that's my best friend, Vick. She was a looker, that Vick was. She was the prettiest of all us before...." Layla's voice trailed off. A tear dropped onto the picture.

Now, that was something I probably needed to ask about, but interrogating a crying woman was not something I was about to do. No way. No how.

She wiped the tear from the picture. "Look at me." She laughed a crying little laugh. "I'm just a sentimental ol' fool, Nicky."

Then she went through every picture in that book. I was there at least three hours—three hours that I could have spent solving the mystery, not listening to an old woman reminisce. But Layla was not just any old woman. In those three hours, I grew to care about her. Hard to believe, but true. She drew you in, and you instantly would do anything for her.

On the next-to-last page of the scrapbook, there was the shot that had been in the newspaper—a picture that Wunnenberg, the reporter, had told me he'd found at the public library.

"Wait. This is the picture that was in the newspaper," I said.

Layla looked at me. "Has that story already been printed? That reporter promised to send me a copy. I don't get the paper, dear. So much sad news in the world, you know."

So Layla didn't have a clue that I had seen this picture before until I told her. That could be to my advantage. I know that sounds conniving, but remember, I had to deceive to get to the bottom of Steve's predicament. A few days before, I had been honest as the day is long. Now the lies and omissions were natural as rain. I guess having a ghost for a boyfriend can do that to you.

"Yes, Layla, this is the picture they printed. I'm certain of it."

"Pretty good body for an old broad like me, huh?" She winked.

I felt a little strange saying it, but I said, "Layla, you're still a beauty." Argh. It was like coming on to my grandmother.

"You're a sweetie, Nicky. I know you don't mean it, but you really know how to pick up an old lady's spirits."

"So," I ventured, "are any of the guys in this picture ones you've told me about?"

She pointed out three of them, giving their names. There was the lighting guy she'd mentioned earlier, the stage manager, and the prop master.

"Who's this?" I pointed at Steve in the picture.

She smiled. "That was my little love." She paused. I just stared at her, waiting for her to go on and hoping I didn't look anxious. I couldn't blow this.

"That, honey, was Vick's little boy. He was as cute as a button when he was a baby. I bet I changed more diapers on that baby than his own mother did."

"He looks like he's about my age in this picture." I wanted to keep her talking, keep her telling me everything she could about Steve. Or—it suddenly flashed across my mind—someone who looked a lot like Steve. Layla could clear everything up for me.

"Oh, he was. But he will always be my baby."

Sounded like she talked to this guy every day.

"So you still have contact with him?" This was getting stranger. Maybe Steve *was* bullshitting me about it being him in that picture.

"Nicky, darlin', that's one of my great regrets. I lost contact with Stevie. I haven't seen him since the night the Palace closed."

Stevie. Truth time. "Really? He must be in his thirties now. Surely you could track him down."

"I tried, sweetie," she said. "I hired the best detectives in the world, but they never found a trace of him. Maybe my little lamb doesn't want to be found."

"Why in the world would he not want to see you?" I probed more. I was having a hard time wrapping my mind around all this.

"Well, that last night, I overheard him arguing with someone."

Now we were getting somewhere.

She continued. "He'd come to the theater like usual. By that time, Vick was gone. Poor Vick. She'd got into drugs. They were her downfall, I'm afraid."

Drugs? This was something else Steve hadn't mentioned.

"Vick worked in the box office for a while after she quit dancing, but the drug problem just got worse and worse. I felt so sorry for poor Stevie, especially after Vick died. He seemed so lost. But, by that time, he had finished high school—you know, I paid for that Catholic school for him; I had to see my baby get his education. He was getting paid to work at the Palace, and he was living by himself in the apartment Vick had rented. He was becoming a little man, that's what he was." There was such a sweet, sad smile on her face.

"So, if you paid for his school, it seems to me that he would be grateful enough to keep in touch." She had to spill the entire story. I had to know.

"He never knew about that. I told the father who was the principal to tell Stevie that his momma had gotten him a scholarship. No, I didn't want my baby to think any worse about his momma than he must have after she died, you know."

"So, you say the last time you saw him he was having an argument?"

"Sure was. His little boyfriend—George, his name was—followed him to work."

I don't know what the expression on my face showed, but Layla looked at me and said, "Don't look so shocked, Nicky. You young people today are supposed to be a lot more accepting than they were in those days. I knew about Stevie by the time he was twelve. We had a lot of homosexuals in the theater, darlin'."

"So, this guy—his boyfriend—who was he?" How could I be jealous of a boyfriend Steve had had over twenty years ago? But I was. And, of course, knowing his name could help solve the puzzle.

"Well, just because I knew about Stevie doesn't mean he ever told me anything about what went on between him and that young man. I didn't even know the boy's name until that last night. I can only tell you that that cute little sports car the boy drove had a parking sticker on it that said Mervyn Industries. But if he worked there, he wasn't just any old person on the assembly line, I tell you. That boy had money."

"Mervyn Industries? You mean the place over on Throckmorton?"

"Are they still in business?" she asked. "I haven't been to that side of town in years."

"Oh yeah," I said. "They're still there."

Shit a brick. The president of Mervyn Industries was none other than George Mervyn III. I knew that because his wife was one of the

Streetwise Players' biggest benefactors. I'd seen her at countless productions. I didn't tell Layla that. Another omission. *I'm going to hell.*

"Well, anyway," Layla said, "Stevie and his young man were having a huge altercation. The kid was absolutely furious at Stevie.

"'Steve,' he shouted, 'how could you do this to me?'

"Stevie told him to keep his voice down, but I could still hear them. Stevie said, 'He has to know sometime, George.'

"Then the boy said, 'But he's threatening to disown me.'

"And Stevie said, 'That's the price you have to pay to be free, George.'

"'That's easy for you to say,' the boy shouted. 'You don't have any money anyway. I'm never going to forgive you for this, Steve.'

"And then," Layla said, "he stormed out of the theater. Stevie ran out after him. By that time, I was getting ready for the show. I figured I'd see Stevie after the show, but I never did. It tore me apart. My Sam was waiting for me at the end of the last show. I looked for Stevie, but I couldn't find him. And Sam was tuggin' at me, wanting to go eat. Sam loved his porterhouse steaks." Layla heaved a big sigh. "The closing of the Palace, the end of my dancing career, and I lost my little boy, all in the same night. That George must have broken my little boy's heart for Stevie to run off like he did. I just hope with all my heart that my baby found love eventually. He deserved that so much."

It was time to change the subject before Layla got sad again. Or sadder. I couldn't stand that.

"Can I have another one of those cakes? They're great."

Layla smiled. "Two great minds think alike, huh, sweetie? These are scrumptious, aren't they?" She put another cake on my plate, then rang a bell. The butler appeared, and she told him to wrap up a cake for me to take home.

I sat eating the second cake while Layla put away the scrapbook. "Oh, Nicky, if you only could have seen me dance." She swayed around the room.

"I'm sure you were really something, Layla," I said, spitting crumbs. I grabbed a napkin, saying, "Sorry."

"That's okay, sweetie. It's so much fun having a young person in this house. I only wish my Stevie were here again."

I almost told her, and then I thought, *yeah sure. Like she's going to believe me that Steve haunts the old theater she loved so much.* No, it was best for me to just leave her to her memories.

I looked at my watch and stood. "I really have to be going. It's been a lot of fun, Layla, and you've really helped me a lot."

She rushed across the room and hugged me. "Now you come back to see me, Nicky. Don't be a stranger." She kissed me on the cheek.

I hated myself then, total and utter hatred. I was despicable for using this beautiful soul for my purposes. I couldn't tell her, though. I simply couldn't. There were no words to convince an old woman that her lost boy was a ghost.

I turned to leave.

"Nicky, wait." I turned back. "Don't forget your cake." And she handed me the bundle the butler had brought in.

When I got in the car, I took a deep, deep breath. This was too much to take in. Could the George who had argued with Steve be the current president of Mervyn Industries? And what did that argument mean? Sure, it was obvious that George was pissed because Steve must have somehow outed him to his father. But was he pissed off enough to kill Steve?

I needed to talk to Steve, but it was already after seven. The cast was having a midweek line reading that night. That meant the theater would be full of people, and I knew from experience that Steve would never show himself unless we were alone.

I guessed I was in for another sleepless night.

CHAPTER 12

THERE I was, tossing and turning, because my phantom boyfriend had had another boyfriend before me. *Over twenty years before me.*

Now, that just blows big chunks, don't you think?

I know it's crazy, but Steve was my first. And I couldn't get the thought out of my mind that I wasn't *his* first.

But if what Layla had told me was true—and why would she lie?—then Steve had been carrying on before me with someone else. Not just someone, either. George Mervyn III, respected citizen, loving husband, and... a big old closeted fairy.

How I was going to act on this news was anybody's guess. I had to talk to Steve. But first, I had to get through a whole day of school, that necessary evil that would lead to graduation and freedom. I'd finally gone to sleep, so I was feeling a little better than I had the past several days, but the anxiety of needing to talk to Steve would make it a long, long school day.

Thank Dionysius I have no friends. There was no "Nick, let's go to Mickey D's," or "Nick, you headed to KK with the gang?" Sad me. But it did make it easy to get away from school.

The last bell rang. I shot out of there. And I don't think my tires touched the pavement as I sped to the Laughton. Luckily one of our city's finest didn't pull me over.

I had no sooner shut the door than Steve was all over me. This was getting to be habit with him. A habit I was glad he'd cultivated. At least, last week I was glad.

Like usual he hugged me from behind, spun me around, and tried to kiss me. But I was having none of it. I thought of George, and I went ballistic: a cold, calm, calculated ballistic.

"I talked to Layla," I said, staring him down.

"Layla? How did you know about Layla?"

"A reporter at the *Trib* put me on to her. Why didn't you tell me about her?"

"Layla didn't have anything to do with what happened to me, Nick." His voice had a *lay off Layla* tone. What was that about?

I kept at him.

"You didn't tell me she was almost like a mother to you—that she loved you almost as much as your own mother."

Steve looked away. "I didn't think it mattered. And it hurts too much to think about her."

I put my hand on his shoulder and gently caressed his cheek. To put him off-kilter. He was being too controlled here. I had to crack him.

It worked.

After a while, his face brightened. In fact, he tried to pull me closer to him. "What did Layla say?"

Then the bomb.

"Does the name George Mervyn ring a bell?" Even I heard my resentment.

He dropped his arms.

"George?" Steve asked. The fake innocence plastered across his face told me everything.

"Yeah…. George, as in son of George Mervyn Jr., as in heir to Mervyn Industries, as in your *former* boyfriend? *That* George?"

I had him. I had disintegrated any semblance of masquerade in him. He was totally and utterly guilt ridden.

"Yeah," he said quietly, then walked away.

I followed him. He wasn't walking away from this. It wasn't that easy. He'd asked for my help, and he had to tackle the big stuff or that help was not coming.

"You didn't tell me about him. Were you two lovers? Or just friends?" I knew the answer, but I wanted to hear it from Steve's lips.

"We were lovers," he spat, but then he quickly added, "But I never had the same feelings for him that I have about you. I hope you know by now that what we have is deep."

"When were you going to tell me about him, Steve? Were you going to wait until we had sex, then compare your two lovers? Throw it up to me that George Mervyn was better than me?" I didn't know where this was all coming from, but it was just spilling over, gushing out of me.

"I wasn't going to tell you about him, for sure. That was another life… literally. I'm with you now. And when we finally do get horizontal, you'll be great, I know." He ran his fingers down my cheek. Spiders. "Besides, George broke up with me."

"Broke up with you? That's a little mild, don't you think?" I was angrier than I've ever been. I'd thought I needed to know about George to solve the mystery, but it was pretty obvious that was the furthest thing from my mind. I was experiencing a full-blown jealous rage.

"Huh?" Steve looked puzzled.

"The way Layla tells it, you said something to his father that George was extremely upset about."

"I swear—I didn't say anything to George's dad. He walked in on us. The old man about burst a blood vessel. 'No son of mine is a fucking fag,' he screamed. That old fart chased me out of their house, screaming that he'd have me arrested for, like, trespassing if he ever saw me around again."

"So why did George come to the theater to see you?" I was still pushing it, determined to make Steve admit something to prove that he and George were somehow different than him and me.

"George spazzed out. He blamed me. He said if I hadn't made so much noise when we were together in his room, then his old man would never have suspected anything."

"That's kind of whack, don't you think? Blaming you for his getting caught?"

"I thought so too, but George was freaked. You see, George was a rich kid, one of those trust-fund babies who never had to work. He drove a fancy little two-seater, pulled out Daddy's AmEx card for everything, and basically lived a golden life. If his dad disowned him, he would be up shit creek. So, he couldn't blame himself for what happened, and if he blamed *Daddy*, that would just make matters worse. It looks like I was the only one he *had* to blame."

Steve was so distraught after spewing that story that I was melting. It was obvious this George guy hadn't loved Steve. Not like I did.

I wanted to stand there and bask in that revelation, but I had a murder to solve. George had motive.

"So, do you think George was pissed enough to off you?" *Off you?* I didn't know where I'd pulled that from, but it lightened the mood, both mine and Steve's.

He laughed. "You sound like a bad movie, man." Then he paused, turning serious. "That's a good question. I remember we argued—about his dad and everything, but I don't remember anything after that. Do you think George *did* kill me?"

Just then, my cell phone chimed. I wanted to let it go to voice mail, but then the thought flashed in my mind that it might be news about the theater scholarship. I checked the caller ID, and, sure enough, it was the professor. I flipped on the phone.

"Professor?"

"Nick. I've got some news for you."

This was it. I was in—no more engineering.

"Great," I said.

"The committee met this afternoon. Just left my office, in fact."

Steve was motioning to me, wanting to know what the professor was saying.

"What was their decision, sir?" I mouthed to Steve to hold on.

"Well, Nick, looks like you're in. You've been accepted to the program. Congratulations."

That was incredible news, but I didn't hear the word *scholarship*.

"Fantastic news. But the scholarship, sir? What about that?"

There was a moment of silence on the line. Did the call drop? Did we get cut off? The most important news of my life and technology failed me. Sounds ridiculous, but all I could think was *I've got to get a better plan.*

"I'm sorry, Nick. My secretary stepped in with some papers for me to sign. The scholarship? Well, the committee didn't get to that, yet. This is no excuse, really, but one of our members has had a family issue come up, and she didn't get to review all the applications thoroughly enough, she said. So the scholarship decision was tabled until the next meeting."

"And when's that?" Steve must have seen my face fall because he had stepped closer and was rubbing my arm. It felt good.

"Two weeks. Hang in there. I'm not promising anything, but I feel like you have a really good chance. I'll get back to you."

He rang off.

"So, what's the news?" Steve asked.

"He says I've been accepted to the program."

Steve hugged me. "Totally choice." I waited for his "Why so glum, chum?" but instead, he sincerely asked, "So what's eating at you?"

"The committee isn't naming the scholarships until they meet again in two weeks."

"That's okay, that's okay." He kissed me. "You'll get it. I know you will. They need a good lighting man, right?"

"Right." How could I stay mad at someone who cared that much for me? Especially when I was mad over an old boyfriend from over twenty years ago. And also because I was in love with a ghost. Who knew the rules of ghost/mortal love? Ghost/mortal/gay love. That put another spin on it.

Salutatorian of my class, and I sounded like an idiot. Love does crazy things to you.

"You're going to get that scholarship, you're going to stand up to your dad, and you're going to get the education *you* want, not the one your dad wants for you."

I leaned over and gave him a long, slow, gratifyingly wet kiss. But before we let things get out of hand, I said, "I believe you." Then we broke apart so I could look him in the eye. "But first, I have a murder to solve."

"Thanks, man. But...."

"And you need to consider letting me bring Layla here to see you. She loves you, man."

Can ghosts cry? Because I was sure I saw a tear.

"That was a long time ago, Nick. Let it lay, please."

"Well," I said, putting my hand on his shoulder. "You think about it."

"Yeah," he said. "Okay, I will." He walked across the stage and turned. "Now what's our next move?"

"Well, I'm not sure how I'm going to get to him, but I have to see George Mervyn."

"Which one? The old man's probably dead by now. And if he disowned his son, then George III is probably long gone from this town."

"Not the case, my friend. Trey is alive and well, running his father's company."

"Trey?"

"I guess the new name is part of a makeover of sorts. The new George Mervyn III. The straight one."

"Straight? No way."

"*Au contraire*, Stevie—you're gonna love this. His wife... yes, you heard right, his beautiful, society page, trophy wife Belinda... is one of Streetwise Players' biggest supporters."

"Wife?" Steve looked like I had struck him with a baseball bat. "Looks like Georgie ended up selling out after all."

"Yep, it does. And wifey is probably the perfect cover for him. Knowing what I know about *then* and now, I think I'll be able to find out all we need to know from Mr. George 'Trey' Mervyn III, Esquire."

CHAPTER 13

I JUST about sprained my brain trying to think of a way to get in to talk to Trey Mervyn. Then the plan just dropped right into my lap.

Well, actually, it dropped right onto my desk in homeroom. Our school's ace reporter, Josh, handed me the latest issue of our homegrown school newspaper. That rag is usually filled with fluff, but the staffers are proud of it, and it costs nothing to the "subscribers," which is everyone in school.

But I'm getting off track here. I scanned the front page, and there, in big type, was the headline: "Local businessman is Dulles grad." Now, you're thinking that this was a story about Trey Boy, but you're wrong. It featured another of our prominent, richer-than-God citizens.

But here's my point: I would call Mervyn's office, pretend to be on the Dulles newspaper, and arrange an interview. Sweet.

I picked up the bathroom pass from Coach Thompson's desk—my homeroom teacher was a coach, and coaches can't be bothered with writing passes. So I lugged this giant wooden key that had *BATHROOM PASS* burned into it.

Once in the restroom, I pulled out my cell, retrieved the number I had already looked up, and punched in Mervyn Industries.

Electronic voices led me all the way to the president's office. I guess I'd picked up some serious acting skills just watching Streetwise shows, because I put on my gracious-student-reporter-looking-for-a-favor persona, and it worked. I explained to his secretary that our school paper was doing stories on local businessmen, and that I would like to interview Mr. Mervyn.

She set up an appointment, and I was in for that afternoon.

I GOT there exactly on time. I figured a businessman would be impressed with punctuality.

The secretary led me right in, and a tall, imposing man came around the massive desk.

"Fortunati, isn't it?" I nodded. "Trey Mervyn." He offered his hand. After we shook, he motioned for me to sit in the chair facing his desk. Then he meandered back around and sat himself, almost as if he was taking his throne. He had this business-mogul thing down pat. "So, let's begin, shall we?"

I fired off a bunch of questions that I figured he would be expecting: stuff about Mervyn Industries, their position on the stock exchange—see, I did my homework—and, just to impress him, their position on the Fortune 100 Best Places to Work list. I had learned that this list was published every year; the companies on the list were determined from interviewing their employees. In a sense, the employees chose the winners.

Unfortunately, I'd only had time to look up the business stuff. I'd found almost nothing about Mervyn's personal life, which, of course, was what I was there to probe.

I eased myself into those questions, that acting thing really taking hold on me.

"Where did you go to college, Mr. Mervyn?"

"Yale, class of '94." He smiled when he said that, obviously proud. I wanted to puke, he was so officious.

"And high school?"

"St. Pius, over on the north side of town."

"Pius, huh?" Now I had him where I wanted him. It was time to push his buttons. "I know someone who went to Pius." I was proud of myself, the way I managed to just slip that in there. Dionysius, I was good. Calculated plan, but he'd played right into my hands. If he was

Steve's killer, then Trey Boy would choke when I mentioned Steve's name. "He's about your age. Maybe you knew him… Steve Stripling?"

Mervyn's face darkened. I couldn't read it, but there was definitely something there. He became very uncomfortable at the mention of his former lover's name.

"Steve…." He sighed. "I haven't thought of him in years."

Okay—that didn't mean he thought Steve was still alive. He was stalling, I was convinced of that. And two could play that game. Change the subject, get him comfortable again, then plunge the knife a second time.

"How did you meet your wife?" An innocent question. Certainly something a reporter would ask.

"My wife? Belinda?"

"Yes. I volunteer with the Streetwise Players. And your wife is one of their biggest boosters." A little truth; a little deception. This was the way to get to him.

"You're right. She's one of their strongest supporters. But Belinda is not my wife; she's my ex."

I almost lost it. I was not expecting that at all. So much for research. I tried to keep it together by plastering a smile on my face.

"Ex?"

"That's right. I met her at Yale. Beautiful, intelligent, friendly. Belinda's the best. But, unfortunately, I married her before I owned up to who I really am. It made my father happy, but I'm afraid I was a real shit to poor Bel."

He paused, lost in thought for a moment. Then he took a long, deep breath, expelled it, and looked me straight in the eyes. No—he couldn't be coming out to me. People as deep in the closet as he must have been do not come out to strangers—not high-school-reporter strangers.

"Look, Fortunati, I've got some advice for you. Always—and I mean, *always*—be true to yourself. Don't let anyone or anything get in your way of being who you really are."

What was he saying?

"I don't know what you mean, sir," I said. I was being totally honest there.

"Oh, I think you do. I could tell the moment you walked in here."

I looked down at my notepad. Was it that obvious? Did he know that I was gay just from looking at me? I took off my glasses and meticulously cleaned them, digging imaginary gunk from the hinges. Anything to keep from looking at him.

This was emphatically the first time anyone had ever called me on this—had ever seen me for what I am. And it had to be Steve's possible murderer. I didn't know if I wanted to hear what he had to say about me, or if I wanted to safely steer the conversation back to Steve.

That was not my choice to make, though.

"You mentioned Steve Stripling." Another pause, an empty thirty seconds. Steve's name sat on the air, waiting for Trey Mervyn to decide what to do with it.

"Steve Stripling was my first love," Mervyn stated, just as if he had said, "I love french fries," or "The sky is blue."

Did I mention I'd done research before I got there? Looked like there was a ton of info that I hadn't dug up.

"Come again?" I tried hard to pretend that what he was saying wasn't cutting deep into me. I put my glasses back on and looked straight at him, trying desperately to look cool and uninterested.

"You heard me. Steve Stripling was the first man I ever fell in love with." He looked above my head, like he was staring into a memory. "Well, we were just kids, really. But it was so incredible. I was stuck in the closet—I know you know what that means."

I gulped.

"Don't you, Fortunati?"

I nodded so slightly that he may not have seen, but he continued his story. He was more relaxed, like telling it was some sort of monumental release.

"My father was a real hard-ass about gays." I almost blurted out, "Mine too," but I wasn't there to talk about me. Mervyn continued, "He'd made that abundantly clear my entire life. Back in those days, being gay was something that was hush-hush. Nobody was out. If Father even got a whiff that one of his employees was gay, he'd fire him right on the spot. No, there was no way I could tell Father that his own son was gay."

Why not twist that knife as you plunge it in, Trey? No—he had no way of knowing that he was telling my life story in tandem with his.

"So Steve and I kept it all a secret." Another pause, but this time it was more like he was just collecting his thoughts, not groping for what to say. "But secrets have a way of coming out. Father caught us one day, alone in my room. Steve was a very vocal lover. Father heard him and stormed in.

"All hell broke loose. Father was livid, making all kinds of threats. Told Steve to leave, and—just like a cheesy old movie—said, 'Don't ever darken this door again.' Father was a piece of work, that man was."

I heard shades of regret, sadness.

"The last time I ever saw Steve was at the old Laughton Theater. He worked there. Ironic, huh? I had one of the worst experiences of my life where you work now."

I was beginning to like the guy and to feel sorry for him. I just couldn't believe he was responsible for Steve's death. But maybe that *worst experience* was the murder of his lover, so I sat and let him talk.

"In those days, the place was a strip joint. A good Catholic schoolboy like Stevie worked at a strip joint."

Finally, he was getting to the climax of his tale. Would the confession come that I was hoping for so I could help Steve? And what would happen when I did help Steve? No—I put that thought away. I'd promised to do what I could for him, and this was what I was doing.

"So, when Father chased Steve out of our house, I followed him to work. I was furious. I was convinced that Father would cut me off. I was young and stupid and thought that money was everything in those days. Having no money terrified me. I told Steve that, but he just said, 'The truth has set you free' or something like that. I was furious at him because I wouldn't let myself be furious at me. And all Steve did was spout a stupid cliché. I thought it was bullshit then, so I stormed out. Steve came after me, but I was boiling over. I guess, deep down, I knew how much I loved him because as mad as I was, I wanted to get out of there. Maybe I thought if I stayed, I'd do something I'd really regret."

What?

"Out in the lobby, Steve was trying to get me to stay when a goon came out of the office. He told Steve that the boss—that's what he called the guy who ran the place—wanted to see him… something about missing ticket money. Steve turned to talk to the guy, and I left. All he said to the guy was 'not now.' But that was time enough for me to leave."

George "Trey" Mervyn III, society patron and business giant, was wasted. The telling of his story had deflated him like a popped balloon.

And I was no closer to finding my murderer. Because I believed him.

He sat, silent, for a long, long time. Eventually, he spoke.

"I never saw Steve again."

The heartbreak was audible. I didn't know what to do, to say to him that could make it all right. I had been jealous of him, but now I felt nothing but pity. He had loved Steve—I heard that especially in those five simple words he'd just spoken. But I couldn't help him now. I could only sit until he came up for air.

And eventually that's what he did. A change: Trey Mervyn was once again the composed, confident man he'd been when I first walked into his office.

"But we were talking about my ex-wife. Okay, here's the scoop: Father died during our second year of marriage, and I inherited his stock in Mervyn Industries."

Good. Let's wrap this up. Mervyn, in control and in gear, was ready to finish our interview.

"This company is a high-profile corporation. I realized early on that I could not continue to do what I was doing on the sly without it eventually getting out. So necessity and my love for Bel pushed me out of the closet."

Heavy stuff again. So much for a quick end and quick exit.

"I had kept my hidden life from my wife for two years, but it would all come out sooner or later. Belinda is too good for me to treat her like that. So, I 'fessed up and we divorced. I never looked back."

I wish I'd been a fly on *that* wall. I couldn't find a way to tell my dad about me. How hard would it have been to tell your wife?

"And that's my advice to all young gays locked in their closets…." He narrowed his eyes at me. "Don't waste your life in there. Be honest with yourself and with everyone else."

I'd come here looking for a murderer, and I was getting a lesson in coming out.

"And, Fortunati, it's okay to put all this in your article," he said. "My life is well-known."

Yep, I should have done deeper research. I thought Trey Mervyn was a complete closet case with a wife as his beard. Gay 101: a *beard* is a woman a gay man keeps to convince the public that he isn't gay. Got it? She hides—like a fake beard—who he really is. Boy, was I wrong.

"I'm proud of my life, Fortunati. I head the biggest marriage equality group in the tristate area—this state will legalize gay marriage or I will die trying—and Mervyn Industries has a total nondiscrimination hiring policy. Gay, lesbian, bisexual, or transgender... if you can do the job, you can work at MI. Make sure you put that in your story. Maybe Daddy will read it in hell."

I made a mental note: read the *Tribune* more often. You might learn something, Mr. Salutatorian. If I had, I would have known all about Trey Mervyn.

He looked at his watch, then said, "Anything else you need to know?"

I scanned my yellow legal pad of notes, like I was looking for something else for my *story.*

"No, Mr. Mervyn. I think you've covered it all." I stood. "Thank you for your time, sir."

"Oh, Fortunati. Use my official, for publication, name in your article. But if we meet again, my friends call me Trey. Nickname I picked up when I came out. New me, new name. And after what you've heard from me today, I think we are friends now."

I'd come here wanting to hate him. I ended up in his corner. And feeling lousy. That's two for two: I'd lied to both Layla and Trey. And they deserved better. I hoped to be able to fix things in that regard.

Trey came from around his desk and showed me out of his office.

My mind reeled as I drove to the theater. If Trey Mervyn wasn't our guy, then who was? I was as far up that bowel movement creek as I could get, and it looked like my paddle was nowhere to be seen.

Had I hit a dead end?

CHAPTER 14

THIS THING was getting stranger and stranger. How much deeper was this quandary? Would it ever unravel?

I had thought I could work through this mystery pretty quickly. I usually am good at figuring out whodunit TV shows and crime novels. But this was spinning out of control with its zigs and zags.

First I had the stripper who became a rich dame, then the repressed homosexual who became the poster boy for out and open. Okay, I know I'm sounding harsh here. But that's how I felt when I thought about it all. I wanted to make Layla and Trey sound like potential villains so I could regain perspective and get this solved.

Then Steve gave me an earful about the goon that only confused me more. Nothing was what it seemed.

Turned out the guy I called "the goon" was a mama's boy. If you're like me, you have a mental picture, formed from watching gangster movies. The guy would be slightly overweight, a gun-toting dimwit who would do anything to protect "the boss." Well, think again.

Turns out, the guy's name was Bertrand Coleman—Bert for short—and he lived at home with Mama. Our boy Bert was a thirty-year-old titty-baby. Never left home; never wanted to. His mama needed him. And—I think it's safe to say—he needed Mama, at least that's the conclusion I came to after what Steve told me.

Dionysius. Could it get any weirder?

Now, if Bertie had been thirty back then, that would make him midfifties now. That was all I knew. There was no Bertrand Coleman in the phone book, and googling him turned up nothing. There were only three Colemans in town, apparently, and none of them knew him.

I had hit a brick wall. And, frankly, I was ready to throw in the towel. I loved Steve and wanted to help him. But I couldn't take the pressure.

I mean, think about it. If my purpose in solving this murder, if it was a murder, was to release the soul of my boyfriend (doesn't *that* sound hokey?), then I'd be cutting off my nose to spite my face, as Mom says. I might be doing a good deed for Steve's eternal soul, but I'd also be losing a boyfriend. Let's weigh this: my happiness; Steve's soul.

Okay, okay, I hear you loud and clear. I had to put Steve before myself. That was not only the right thing to do, but that was what, buried deep in me, I wanted to do—whatever the consequences.

But I really didn't know what else I could do. How was I going to find this guy Bert, assuming he was still around?

It was enough to give me a brain drain. I needed a break. Sometimes you think more clearly if you rest a bit and regroup your thoughts. And sometimes, serendipity happens.

Here's how it went down: I had a whole Saturday to put it behind me. You see, I had this class that required community service. No CS, no grade. I was stuck. And to top it off, I had waited until everyone else had signed up. While some were getting to work Habitat for Humanity and others were rescuing animals at the local shelter, I was assigned to the retirement home. I was given the *privilege* of working with a bunch of old people for an entire Saturday.

Don't get me wrong. I love old people. My grandma is old. But spending a whole day with them? Give me a break.

I arrived at Western Hills Assisted Living Center precisely at 7:55 to begin work at 8:00 a.m. sharp. I'd heard tales of Ms. Lampson docking our grades if we were late.

The lady there asked me a bunch of questions, trying to decide where she wanted to put me. One of her questions: Do you play bridge? So, at this point, most of you are asking, "What's bridge?" Well, it's an old person's card game. I'd learned to play it because Gran likes it, and I will do just about anything for my Gran.

A smile popped out on the center lady's face when she found out I played bridge. It seemed she had four old women who played from dawn to dusk every day, and one of them had left with her son that day. So I was drafted to be the fourth at their table.

Okay… here's the drill. Bridge takes a lot of concentration, and these three old ladies were aces at the game. Bridge sharks. In fact, that day of torture I was expecting turned out to be fun. They were great players—almost as good as Gran.

Like I said, there were three of them: Sadie, Maude, and Ruth. Ruth was a hoot. She "cussed like a drunken sailor," as Gran would say, and told great stories in between hands. And she was also the best player of the bunch.

Those three played through lunch. I was starving, but I needed that grade, so I wasn't about to do anything to rock the boat.

Along about four o'clock, this tall guy sauntered into the room. He walked over to the table and gave Ruth a peck on the cheek.

"Don't bother Mama now, Bertie. Can't you see I'm winning?" she said.

Frozen in time. That's the only phrase to describe my reaction.

"Nick. Your turn."

I played my next card, no longer concentrating on the game. Could it be this easy? This guy was about the right age. He fit the description Steve had given me. And from his reaction to Ruth, mama's boy was written all over him.

It looked like Somebody Up There had dropped a gift right in my lap. Serendipity, yeah?

Or karma. About the same thing. Only karma often leads to bad things. And if Bertie was my killer, then his karma had just changed.

This Bertie sat on the sofa near us and picked up a magazine lying on the table. I kept eyeing him, trying to decide if this could be true, and also how I was going to approach him if he was Bert Coleman.

We finished our game. Maude pushed back her chair. "Well, girls, looks like it's almost suppertime, and I need to take a potty break. Do you think Tillie will be back tomorrow for our game?"

"She'd better be," Ruth exclaimed. "She owes me ten bucks."

Sadie turned to me. "Thank you, Nick, for playing with us today. You are a delightful partner."

She stood, came around the table, and hugged me from behind.

"Wait," I said, an idea forming in my head. "My gran loves playing bridge. I'd bet that she'd be happy to come over to be a fourth if any of you have to be out sometime."

"How sweet," Sadie gushed. "Give us her number."

I wrote Gran's phone number on the score sheet. I was getting good at this. Here I was using my dear old grannie for nefarious purposes. But, I told myself, she does love to play bridge. No harm, no foul.

Then I said, "I'll be sure and tell her all about you guys. But it occurs to me that I don't even know your last names."

Maude spoke, pointing to each of them, starting with herself. "Maude Burris, Sadie Bell, and Ruth Coleman...."

I knew it. The thought was so loud in my head that I wondered if I'd said it out loud. But, thankfully, I'd shown more discretion.

Now I'd be able to get at the truth.

I was trying to think of what to say to Bert when I realized Maude was still talking. It took everything I had to concentrate on what she was saying.

Maude continued, "... but you can just call us the Bridge Bees."

I laughed, and Sadie said, "That's what we call ourselves in tournaments."

By this time, Bert had stood and walked over to Ruth. "You ready for supper, Ma?" He reached for her arm.

"Don't rush me, Bertie," she said, pulling away from him. "Please join us, Nick. It's the least we can do after all the attention you've shown us old ladies today. Besides, we made you play through lunch. You have to be ravenous."

And the chance literally dropped into my lap. I could talk to Bert during dinner.

"I'd be delighted, Ruth." My mother would have been proud— that is, as long as she didn't know I was using poor Ruth. Mom had taught me well. No one, but no one, has better manners than me—when I want to use them.

I trailed Bert and Ruth into the dining room, where we sat at a table set for six.

As uniformed waiters poured water—this was evidently a high-class old folks' home—I said, "Bert, is it?"

"Yeah," he said.

"*Yeah?*" Ruth narrowed her eyes at him. "Where are your manners, Bertie?"

He didn't even look disgusted. This guy was whipped.

"I saw a picture recently of a Bert Coleman. Weird. I'm sure it wasn't of you," I said, hoping to get a rise out of him.

"Really?" He had perked up. "Where'd you see it?"

"Well, I volunteer at Streetwise Players. You know—at the old Laughton Theater. There are some old ledgers and pictures there left over from a previous tenant." I was trying to be a little cagey. After all, this guy was so whipped that I'd bet Mama was totally unaware he'd worked in a strip joint. "One of the pictures had names written on the back."

"Bertie used to usher at the Laughton," Ruth announced.

Now, how he kept it from his mother that the Laughton housed a strip show, I couldn't imagine, but apparently he had. Somehow, I don't think Ruth would have been happy that her baby was around titty dancers.

Bert eyed me, a stricken look on his face. "Yeah, it must have been me. All us *ushers* posed once."

I immediately caught his emphasis on the word *usher*. Bertie didn't want Mama to know, even after all these years, just what his involvement was in the old Palace. Mama still thought the place had been a movie theater when Bert worked there, and he wanted to keep it that way.

I could easily go along with that—especially if it meant I'd find out what I needed to know.

A waiter arrived to take our order. We could choose either fish or chicken that night, he announced.

I dropped my line of questioning, figuring I'd get more out of Bert if I could get him alone. I didn't know how that was going to happen, but in a burst of newfound confidence, I knew I would make it happen.

The rest of the meal was spent with Ruth spinning tales of her younger days as we ate. And, I have to tell you, the chicken I ordered was pretty good.

Dessert and coffee were finally served, after which Ruth folded her napkin and stood. "I've got to get back to my room. My shows are starting in ten minutes. Coming, Bertie?"

"I'll walk Nick out," he said. "I'll catch you in a minute, Ma."

Ruth seemed proud that Bertie was being so polite to me. "Good for you, Bertie. Mama taught you well. Come to my room when you finish." The last was not a request; it was a command. She left.

"Mama don't know about the strippers, Nick," Bert said as we walked. "And I'd just as soon keep it that way."

"I got that, Bert. And, believe me, your secret is safe with me. I'm not here to cause you any grief." Here the man was over fifty years old, and he was still afraid of his mommy.

"I understand, Bert," I continued. *"No problema."* I wanted him to think I was his friend. Gain his confidence, gain his confession. "My lips are sealed... but speaking of, how did you keep it a secret from *her*?"

"Mama grew up in the neighborhood where the old theater is. But she married Pop, and they moved clear across town. She had no idea that the old place wasn't showing movies anymore."

"So you just let her think you were an usher?"

"Right... when I was really the strip show's 'go-to' guy. I did a million jobs around there." Bert seemed to be enjoying thinking about his past, and hidden, life. "Them dames loved me."

"I know someone who worked there at that time too." I decided to use the same ploy with Bert that I had used with Mervyn. If Bert had killed Steve—which really didn't seem likely, although stranger things have happened: a mama's boy can go berserk, you know—then he would know I was lying. "Steve Stripling?"

"Stevie?" Bert seemed genuinely happy to hear Steve's name. Looked like I was right about Bert not being a murderer. But maybe he knew who was. "Stevie was a real good kid. It was that mother of his that had the problems."

"Really? The most Steve's ever told me about his mom was that she is dead now."

"Dead from a drug overdose," Bert said. "That gal couldn't stay away from the stuff. That's what got her in hot water with the boss."

"What kind of hot water, Bert?"

"Well, by the time we were closing the theater, Vick was too messed up to strip. She'd lost it, you know. But the boss, he had a soft spot for the girls. So he let Vick sell tickets. She had that boy to support, you know.

"Well, money came up missing. The boss knew Vick had skimmed it off the top of the ticket sales. He was planning to go after her for it. But Vick, she up and died. That money had gone up her nose or right into her veins.

"So, the boss, being the forgiving man he was, decided just to write it off. In fact, the boss called Steve in the last night the theater was open to tell him not to worry about the money Vick took.

"Steve looked shocked, I remember. Not only did he not know about the missing money, but that kid didn't even know what killed his mama. Vick must have hid her problem pretty damn good."

"Wait a minute. Steve would have been about as old as me then. There's no way he wouldn't know if his mother was a drug addict."

"That's what I thought too." Bert nodded. "But Layla and the other girls, they was very protective of little Stevie. Layla found Vick the night she died. She wouldn't let Steve see his mama until the funeral home had fixed her all up."

"But what did she tell Steve?" I asked.

"She told him that his mama had a heart attack. He was real broke up. But he bought it, hook, line, and sinker." Bert scratched his nose. "For a kid who grew up in a strip joint, he was one easy mark.

"Anyway, closing night, the boss told Steve not to worry about the missing money."

So that's why Bertie had distracted Steve and Trey. The boss wanted to see Steve. Could the boss be the murderer? I was overthinking. Of course the boss didn't kill Steve. He was being nice to him, forgiving his mother's debt.

"So what did Steve do then?" I asked.

"He just left the office," Bert said and shrugged. "I guess he went to find Artie, the lighting guy. Stevie was kinda like Artie's assistant, and it was our last show, after all."

"Well, Bert, I'll tell Steve I saw you." I got in my car and rolled down the window.

Bert leaned in. "I'd love to see Stevie again sometime. You tell him that, Nick."

I had to think quick. But I was becoming a proficient liar. And I was also getting good at not worrying about my lies. "I'll tell him to look you up if he ever comes to town again. He doesn't live here anymore."

"Well, okay," Bert said. "Hope you come back here again sometime, Nick. Mama and the girls sometimes need a fourth, and I never could figure out that damned game."

I pulled out of the parking lot, thinking *Okay, was Steve even murdered? Maybe he just died of natural causes. Maybe he offed himself. Maybe he OD'd on some of his mother's drugs.* I was up a blind alley in more ways than one.

CHAPTER 15

WHEN I got home that night, I rummaged through the kitchen cabinet where Mom kept the aspirin. I had a raging headache.

"What are you looking for, Nick?" I heard Mom say from behind me.

I turned around. "Don't we have any aspirin? I have a headache."

I understated how much my head was killing me because God forbid I should have a common, ordinary headache—even a really bad one brought on by stress because I was trying to solve a murder. Mom couldn't buy that. My mom is the ultimate Italian mama, overprotective and totally dedicated to the art of mothering. She immediately pounced on me, feeling my forehead and pounding me with questions.

"Do you have a fever? What does it feel like? A dull ache, or a throbbing? Have you eaten today? Are you sick at your stomach?" You know the drill. Dionysius, she could be a real pain.

By the time Mom had finished her interrogation, the headache was worse, if that was possible.

"Maybe you need new glasses, baby. It's been over a year. I'm calling Dr. Brasher first thing Monday morning." Big leap. Headache equals vision problems. That's my mom.

Which was how I found myself sitting in the exam chair at the optometrist. I really didn't mind, though, because I knew I'd get new glasses out of this deal, and my old frames were showing a lot of wear. I was hard on glasses.

Doc Brasher was just finishing.

"Quite a change, Nick. Have you not been wearing your glasses?"

"Most of the time." From the first time he'd seen me, when I was twelve, he'd been on me to wear my glasses all the time. But I hated those things, and despite my sucky vision, I really did go without a lot. Not when I was driving or having to read the board in class, but I'd say they were off as much as they were on. That's how much I despised them. I was willing to walk around blind rather than let people see me in my glasses. Sad me, huh?

"Uh-huh," he said, writing on his prescription pad. "That means 'not much,' doesn't it, Nick?"

"Well," I said, hoping to appease him, "when I drive and when I watch TV."

"Nick, my man." Doc Brasher always wanted to sound like your best friend. "This is a significant change." He handed me the prescription. "And it's time now for you to wear them all the time. That means put them on when you get up and don't take them off until you go to bed. You understand?"

Busted. Maybe I'd like my new frames better.

"Yes, sir," I said.

"I guarantee things will be a lot clearer with these new lenses," he declared.

I cursed under my breath as I made my way to the optical shop next door. There was no way I was going to wear those things all the time. No way. Not even if I got frames that made me look like a movie star. Yeah, like how many movie stars show themselves in specs?

I was looking around, waiting for someone to help me. I did a few try-ons. I didn't like anything, but then again, I never liked picking out new frames. I was staring at my old, beat-up frames, wondering if I could just have new lenses put in them. I decided that was an impossible move, so I kept fruitlessly looking around. I'd have to get really close to the mirror just to see my face clear enough to figure out what I looked like. Dionysius, this was proving to be a wasted and frustrating afternoon.

I had just slipped a pair of Armanis on when I heard a familiar voice.

"Nice frames," he said.

I looked around, and there stood Wash Vitek. You remember Zach's nephew—the gorgeous guy Zach'd slyly fixed me up with on opening night.

I instinctively ripped off the Armanis. Like he'd not noticed them already. Like he didn't already know I wore glasses. What was wrong with me?

"Wash. What are you doing here?"

He twirled around in his white coat.

"Oh, you work here," I said. And a hint of red must have crept into my face. I can be such a dork.

"Well, for all you know, I just came here from my job as a butcher at the grocery store. They wear white coats too," Wash said. "Or maybe I just took a break from my job as a handler in the loony bin." I felt my face getting hotter. He seemed to be loving it. "Or it could be that I demonstrate cosmetics over at Macy's." He let me stand there, stewing in my embarrassment.

Then he let out a belly laugh. "Quit your blushing, Nick. Yes, I work here. Associate of the month, three months running." He proclaimed that proudly. I had no idea he sold glasses.

"Well," I said, internally commanding my blush to go away, "it's great to see you again." I was such a douche. I fawned over him. Dionysius.

"Likewise," he said, charm oozing. I found myself stirring a little *down there*, if you know what I mean.

To avert disaster, I quickly got down to business. I couldn't let Wash see me like that, and besides, I told myself, he's not gay, I am, and I love Steve. I handed Wash my glasses and the new scrip. "I need these new lenses. You can do it in an hour, right?"

Wanting to get out of there, I'd forgotten that my old frames were not likely to hold up to new lenses.

Wash looked at the piece of paper, then looked at my glasses.

"Nick, I'm not going to lie to you. There are one-hour places out there, but we're not one of them. We can fit people's old frames with new lenses all the time, but these crummy frames are almost falling apart. They might not last on you, and of course, while we're working on them, you'd be without glasses for at least a week, which would not be a good thing. Trust me. Why not let me help you with a smokin' new look?"

I was stuck. I couldn't do without. It was either let Wash help me, or find a one-hour place. Then I'd be back to having to decide on new frames all by myself. So I gave in to him.

He sat me down, and for the next thirty minutes, Wash helped me pick out new frames.

I never knew someone could make picking out new glasses into a party. We laughed and laughed. Wash first started with frames that there wasn't a chance I would be caught dead in. He made me try on blue frames, red frames, orange frames, all the time insisting that they looked sexy on me.

He slid a pair of blue-and-white plastics on my ears and said, "These are the ones, Nick. The chicks'll go wild over them."

There was a look on his face that I couldn't quite read, but I instantly jerked the frames off, thinking *Yeah, just what I always wanted*, and a warmth came over me. Wash was just doing his job and here I was, getting all hot and bothered over him. Why was I so maladjusted?

"I don't think the rainbow colors are for me, Wash. They're just not my thing, you know." I laughed when I said it, trying to get the mood back to the party and away from my swelling *self*-awareness.

"I get ya, Nick… more the conservative type. No prob," he said, pulling a bunch more off the wall—the blacks, the grays, the metals, the rimless—and brought them back to the desk.

Maybe since I was getting hotter as time passed, it seemed like he recommended hundreds of different looks. With each one, he carefully placed the frame on me. And with each new try on, he'd brush my forehead or I'd feel his warm breath graze my cheek.

It had been a long time since I'd bought glasses, but I didn't ever remember the process turning me on. This was new to me indeed.

Wash's fingertips gently slid over my cheeks as he removed his latest recommendation. I silently gasped, squirming a bit in the chair. *Get a grip*, I thought. *He's only doing his job.*

He looked at me and smiled. Did he know what was going on with me? *No*, I told myself, tugging at my jeans under the table, trying to make more room. *He's just being a good salesman—a* very *good salesman.*

He held up another pair. "l.a. Eyeworks—the absolute best we carry. All the hunks in Hollywood wear these. *Perfect* for you, Nick, you hunk."

Talk like that would get him somewhere. No doubt he was selling his wares. But at that point, if his wares included a somethin' somethin', I wouldn't have turned it down.

He slid the l.a. Eyeworks on me, leaning over to check that the earpieces were snug. His gorgeous eyes were two inches from mine, his luscious lips almost touching me, and I was about to explode.

He sat back and pointed to the mirror. I was so under his spell that I forgot for a moment why I was there.

Looking in the mirror, I had to admit that they looked great on me. But at that point, I would have chosen anything just to get out of there, get away from the torture Wash was inflicting—that I was inflicting on myself because I was sure Wash had no idea what his effect on me was.

"Watch out, Hollywood, here comes Nick," Wash joked as I handed him the credit card, the one Mom had put in my name with a stern "only for emergencies." She knew I was here, so using the card wasn't a problem, but I would also classify getting out of there as quickly as possible an *emergency.*

As he rang up the sale, Wash said, "You'll be fighting off the talent scouts in these." I was sure he said something like that to all his customers.

I was feeling drained when I left the shop, but, sitting in my car, safely away from Wash's bewitchment, I found myself actually looking forward to getting his call in a week or so when my new glasses were in. Wash had made me believe that I actually looked good in them.

I couldn't wait to tell Steve about it all—well, about the new glasses part, not about the Wash turning me on part. Dionysius, I wasn't stupid.

The theater was dark when I got there. That was a good sign that Steve might be waiting. He did like his alone time with me.

"Where've you been, lover?" He greeted me with open arms as soon as I stepped through the door.

"I had to go to the eye doctor." I told him all about my appointment and about the new glasses. I omitted any reference to Wash Vitek, remembering how jealous Steve had been the night I met Wash.

Steve said, "I'm sure you'll look sexy in those fresh specs. But then again, you always look sexy."

I changed the subject.

"So," I said, "I met Bert Coleman."

"What? Good ol' Bert's still around? I thought he'd be long gone."

"Funny thing…." And I related the tale of the Great Bridge Game on Saturday.

"Weird. Who'd have thought that would happen?"

"Tell me about it," I said. "It's like God—or whoever—wants us to find out the answer to all this."

"So, what did you find out, babe? Or do I not want to know?" Steve looked worried.

"Well, Bert didn't kill you, I'm sure of that."

"I never thought he did."

"And you couldn't have told me that the other day? I went after him thinking he might have taken you out."

"Whoa, Nick. You're sounding more and more like a bad cop show." He pecked me on the cheek. "I'm sorry. I thought you got the idea that Bert was one of the good guys."

"Steve, just because he's a mama's boy doesn't mean he couldn't be a killer. But I know now he's not one, so, it's a good thing I didn't go in there accusing him and all."

"Yeah, you're right. So, it all worked out okay, then. Now, what did he tell you?"

"He told me that the guy who owned the place was okay with the missing money. Said he told you not to worry about it."

"Yeah… yeah… that sounds right. I've got a vague memory." He seemed pleased at remembering, no matter how fleeting the memory was.

I gulped, because now I had to bring *it* up. "Why didn't you tell me that your mom OD'd?"

"Mom OD'd?" You'd think I'd hit him with a two-by-four. That's exactly why I hadn't wanted to bring it up. I knew he didn't remember, and this would devastate him. Which it did. But, strangely, only for a moment.

And then, suddenly, it was like a lightbulb flashed over his head.

"Yeah, Mama had a problem." His voice had a slight tremble in it. "I didn't know anything about it. She managed to hide it pretty good. And Layla and the other girls protected her. And me. I swear, when Mama died, Layla told me it was a heart attack, and I believed her. It was only later that I found out about the drugs." Hard speech to make, but he got through it.

I didn't say anything. I had to let him work it all out for himself. Finally, he stopped, and with the palms of his hands, he wiped tears from his eyes. It was then, and only then, that I felt like I could continue questioning him.

"When? When did you find out, Steve? It may help us. Think."

"I don't have to think. I know. I didn't find out the truth until that last night," Steve went on. "Mr. Baumgartner let it slip when he told me about the money."

"Steve, you told me Trey—George—was your last memory of then," I said.

His eyes widened. "You're right." He put his fingers to his forehead. "I guess I just remembered some more, huh?"

"Yes, Steve, I guess you did."

He rubbed his temples. "This is so strange. It's like something buried in a deep, deep hole just floated to the surface."

The look in his eyes was almost frightening; he seemed so confused.

"I think they call that 'recovered memory,'" I said, hoping to ease his anxiety.

Gently, I added, "Steve, if you remember that much, what else do you recall?" I was pushing for more before the memories could leave, but I didn't want to scare them away.

He was silent a long, long time. Then he shook his head back and forth, back and forth. "Nothing else. That's it."

I decided to go at it a different way. Bert had said that Steve must have gone to see the lighting guy after he left the office.

"Do you remember seeing Artie?"

"The college student who was the lighting tech? I must have. Lighting was one thing I did there. I liked doing it. So Artie and I saw each other all the time."

"What about?" I probed.

"You know… lighting stuff, college—he said he might could get me a work-study at the university when I graduated."

"Okay, think now… did you say anything different to Artie that night?"

"Different? I don't think so. We didn't talk much. I mainly just followed his orders."

"Now, think… was there something that had nothing to do with lighting?"

Steve spat the word. "Shit. Artie was my mom's dealer; that's what I found out that night."

CHAPTER 16

STEVE TREMBLED, reliving that night. My heart ached for him. I was supposed to be helping him, yet I was just giving him grief. I could only hope that it would be worth it. He was killing me.

I gently took his hand and led him to a sofa that was backstage. He seemed lost, not really knowing what to do. I sat, pulling him down beside me.

For a long time, we didn't speak. Finally, Steve erupted.

"God damn him." He balled his fists, like he wanted to strike out—strike out at a man who was more than twenty years in his past.

"Steve," I said quietly, "get a grip." I took his fist and tried to pry the fingers apart. This tension was not doing us any good. He was miserable, and I was afraid he would shut down again, and I'd be once again powerless to help him. "I know you're mad, but your anger is not going to help us find this guy."

He jerked his hand away from me. "That bastard did it." You'd think he'd punch the air and shout something like that to the heavens. But it was a whisper. A cold, anguished whisper.

He stood and walked across the stage. I couldn't read him, but I had to find out more, else this realization was all in vain.

"Did what?" I followed him, a step behind, approaching with caution. Nothing should set him off. I needed to talk, rationally and clearly. "Killed you? Tell me what he said to you that night."

"I can't remember his exact words, Nick. He admitted he sold drugs to my mama. I do remember that." Steve was at the stage door by then. "I've got to find him." But the door wouldn't open. Not for Steve.

I turned him around; a look of total defeat creased his face. "I forgot," he said, his voice pitifully quiet. "I can't leave here."

I started to take him in my arms, to caress the hurt from him. I felt his pain and frustration as deeply as he did.

But then his face brightened. Not a full-blown smile. Not a sea change in mood. But a gentle calm was there.

"You've got to find him, Nick," he said. "It's our only hope." And there was a steely look of determination in his eyes. "I'll make him pay."

How could I refuse him? My lover had been through hell. We were now on a path, a path that, of the two of us, only I could physically travel.

"Okay, tell me everything that happened that night," I said.

"That's just it." He hung his head. "I still don't remember."

"But you just said he did it."

"He did—he turned my mom into a drug addict. She never touched that stuff until he came along."

Another roadblock? What I thought Steve was saying and what he truly was saying were two very different things. Was Artie just a lowlife drug dealer, or was he a murderer? Had we hit another dead end? Steve still couldn't tell me what had caused his death that night or who was really involved.

"My mom was beautiful, man. She had creamy white skin and long, silky jet-black hair. And when she danced, you'd swear you were being visited by an angel."

I tried to picture the woman he was describing. Discounting the juiced-up part and the stripper part, he could have been talking about my mom. Do you have to be brought up to be a loving mother, or is it a chemical change that happens once you know you are growing a human life inside you? I made a mental note to tell my mother how much I loved her and appreciated her. Steve had never gotten the chance.

"That asshole got her hooked. Oh, she hid it well... from me, anyway. I guess she was just my mom, and I couldn't see the ways she had changed."

"You loved her, Steve." I caressed his arm. "You weren't capable of seeing the bad, only the good." I pulled him to me and held him for a moment.

"I only wish I'd had a chance to really make her know how much I loved her. Just one more chance. But Artie took that away from me. You've got to find the guy, Nick," Steve said, pulling away. "He's got to pay for what he did to my mom."

"I promise," I vowed. "What's his name?"

"Artie… Artie…." Steve was groping for the name. "Damn. I don't think I ever knew his last name."

"So, describe him, can you? What did he look like? How old was he?"

"I remember he wasn't much older than I was. A college student, like I said before." Steve paced as he talked. "Bertie always called him Beta Phi. Maybe that was a fraternity he was in, I don't know."

"That's good. That's something to start with. Anything else?"

"Tall, redhead. Had a mole just to the side of his eyebrow… ugly-looking thing, that mole. I always wondered why he didn't have it taken off." Steve took a deep breath, then let it out with a huge huff. Then he dropped the F bomb, loud and clear. "It's all coming back now. He was at the university, in the theater program—studying lighting. That's why he was working here. But I guess the Palace didn't pay enough, so he supplemented by dealing…." He shuddered.

I took in all Steve had to say, and a picture leapt into my mind—a portrait I'd seen hanging somewhere—somewhere I'd been recently.

Now it was my turn to shudder.

I saw, clearly before me, a portrait hanging in the lobby of the university theater building: Dr. Arthur Baker, professor of stage lighting. The man I would be answering to if I got that scholarship.

CHAPTER 17

DIONYSIUS! COULD my life suck any worse? Having a ghost for my first boyfriend was bad enough, but now this. I had my dad's hot breath wafting down my back, pushing his precious engineering scholarship. And I thought I'd seen a way out of that, what with the theater scholarship and all. Then, I'd found out that possibly—no, quite probably—the professor I would be working the most closely with was a drug dealer and maybe a murderer.

So, I could do nothing and let this all resolve, hopefully, in my favor. I could win the theater scholarship, tell Dad to go to hell, and live happily ever after. That's if I could live with myself for not exposing a criminal and making my dad a very unhappy camper. Did I really want to do that to the world's greatest dad (with his huge blind spot, of course)?

Or I could keep digging, lay out a case against Professor Baker, lose the theater scholarship, and release my boyfriend from his eternal entrapment in a drafty old theater.

But did I want him released? After all, if I did prove Professor Baker a killer, then Steve would go on to the great whatever, and I would, once again, be alone, heart-numbingly alone. A ghost in the theater is worth two in heaven, know what I mean?

But—and I'm not trying to get all religious here—everyone deserves to go into the light, as they say, and not be trapped forever on Earth.

I know, it sounds like a made-for-TV movie on some obscure cable channel.

But it was *my* movie. Believe me; it was a lot easier when I was this lonely, confused homo who only functioned when his nose was buried in a book or when he was up on a ladder adjusting lights. Why did I ever wish for a boyfriend? And why couldn't I have found one the normal way? Maybe an online ad. Or, of course, I could have not been chickenshit and gone to Met Youth. Surely there would have been someone there for me. But, no, I had to take the easy way out and fall in love with the first boy who seemed interested.

Well, that made me laugh. What was *easy* about any of this? My boyfriend was an out-of-body experience. I had vowed to release his soul. Maybe—just maybe—I was headed for mental hospital hell for buying into any of this.

Why did I care? After all, this was my life I was playing with. Dad wouldn't be living it for me, so the theater thing was my best chance at happiness. So what if one of my teachers had once dealt drugs. That was a long, long time ago. I'd bet—as they say on TV—that the statute of limitations on that crime had run out already.

Now, murder?—that was another thing. But, then again, who knows if Steve had really been murdered? Maybe he had just died. Some horrible accident had occurred that night that made him block his last memories. Yeah—that could be it. Steve had fallen in front of a moving bus. Steve had slipped on ice and hit his head. Steve had taken pills because his mom was a druggie. Any of those things could have happened.

But if that was the case, then where was his body? Wouldn't someone have found it? Then again, if Baker killed Steve, there still would have been a body. What would he have done with it?

This was getting to be a real pain. Here I was, doing my best TV police detective trying to figure out a crime that involved... what? A ghost that only I could see and talk to.

Yep. That hospital was right around life's corner. There was no way this was happening, not to me. Not to Nick Fortunati, honor student, theatrical lighting whiz, and all-round good guy. I could not—I repeat, I *could not* be talking to a phantom, much less be in love with one.

No, it was just not happening. I was hallucinating. Something about the Laughton had made me insane.

Maybe I was so far in the closet that I was no longer living in the real world. I had invented an imaginary boyfriend, one who could never leave me. One that couldn't leave my little world, period. My fantasy had become my reality; I had invented what I wanted for myself.

But was anything in my life what I wanted? A father who wouldn't listen to me, a boyfriend whose kisses made me ache but wanted me to let him leave, and the most insane thing of all: I was chasing after an almost nonexistent scholarship so I could study under a drug dealer/murderer.

The passenger seat next to me buzzed. I jumped, the rumble jerking me out of my thoughts, but I wondered what I was hearing. "This is getting weirder and weirder," I said out loud, looking for the source of the strange sound. My eyes lit on my phone, there on the seat beside me. It was on vibrate. I picked it up just after it stopped. I looked at the readout: University Theater Department.

As if things couldn't get any worse. Was I going to have to face my demons head-on?

I put the phone back on the seat. Whoever was calling would leave a voice mail. I couldn't face anything just yet.

I kept driving. Denial is a good thing.

Ignoring the thing didn't keep my mind from reeling, though. So I put my mind on autopilot, and it decided to review the situation, no matter how hard I shouted *no, no* to it.

I went back to the beginning. I was in the storage room, pulling lamps. I heard a voice....

On overload, my mind finally let me concentrate on my driving. I focused and found that I had driven clear across town. I could have killed someone. I could have killed myself. Then again, was that a bad thing? Maybe I could be Laughton-trapped with Steve. Just kidding. I have no serious suicidal thoughts. Not even to settle the conundrum of my life. No, thank Dionysius the streets weren't busy.

I needed coffee to clear my head. I noticed a Koffee Kart just up ahead, so I pulled in.

I found a big, overstuffed chair in the corner and sat with my steaming cup. I pulled my glasses off and rubbed my eyes. Then I took a sip. The burn of the coffee felt good going down. I cleared my mind, concentrating on the caffeine rush. I breathed... for the first time that day, it felt like. In, out... in, out. Each dose of oxygen seemed to relax me. I felt my body melt into the cushions of the chair.

And then I thought of Steve... Steve touching me, Steve hugging me, Steve kissing me. Steve was real—he might have been a ghost, but he was a *real* ghost. I wasn't crazy, as wigged-out as it seemed. Steve existed, he had been wronged, he was trapped, and he was miserable. I'd seen the hurt in his eyes, the abject hopelessness of being forever caught in a world he no longer belonged in.

Yes, I did think he loved me, but that wasn't enough. As long as he was held prisoner in the Laughton, we couldn't really be together. That was no life for him; it was just existence.

And my own life had taught me that mere existence isn't enough.

I had to help him. I had to solve this mystery.

Even if it meant I would have to give him up to set him on his path.

Yeah—it sounds like I'd suddenly become one of those meditating, yoga-loving weirdos, but that's what I needed to do... release Steve from this world so he could go on to the next.

If I only knew how I was going to do that. The conundrum was going to have to wait, though, because I was so exhausted that I couldn't think straight. I needed downtime, just me, my coffee, and Met Youth. I opened my laptop. Not to be—

I felt a buzz in my shorts. My phone.

I slipped my glasses back on. Then I pulled my phone from my pocket and looked at the readout.

The call was from Dad.

"What's up?"

"The committee wants to see you—tomorrow."

Damn. Were things moving that fast? All I wanted was to be left alone. Why had I taken this call? But I did, so I had to face whatever came.

"What do they want?" I reluctantly asked.

"I wasn't told. But I did hear that they were mighty impressed with you at the company picnic. I knew going to that could only help you, Nick."

I was sunk.

"You still there, Nick?"

"Yeah, Dad. I'm here. I was just trying to remember what might have impressed your buds at the picnic."

"Well, apparently, it was the way you hung with the younger kids. The boss's wife was blown away. She said it showed—and I quote—'a sensitive side that was very appealing.' And you know how he listens to her."

A sensitive side? I had only been hanging with the younger kids because I don't much like people my own age. We never have anything to say to each other. I don't follow football or basketball or whatever sport is in season, and, believe me, the average American teen male has no interest in the theater.

Besides, what does sensitivity have to do with bioengineering? Pushing test tubes around doesn't require much heart.

"So, Dad, when and where is this meeting?" I was feeling totally trapped. I hoped Dad didn't hear it in my voice.

"Tomorrow night... seven. Here, in the boardroom. Try to work up some enthusiasm before then, huh?" Busted. Dad paused. "And Nick, dress up in the suit I bought you, huh?"

"Sure, Dad."

I flipped the phone shut, feeling like my world had crashed and burned. I sat, staring at the phone mindlessly, the screen blurring. I felt a headache coming on.

I took another sip of coffee and longed for the trance I'd found myself in just a little while before.

I focused on the phone, letting the screen hypnotize me, flashing on and off, on and off. Then it registered—the blinking light was telling me I had a message.

I pushed buttons until I heard the voice of Dr. Nichols: "Nick, please call me. This is urgent."

I pushed the callback button.

"Theater Department."

"Dr. Nichols, please. Nick Fortunati here."

"One moment, please."

"Nick, I'm so glad you rang back. I've got incredible news. A new scholarship was just funded for next year. An alumnus—I can't tell you his name, but I will say he's designed lights for some pretty giant Broadway hits—has specified that the moneys go to someone who plans a lighting concentration. I, of course, immediately thought of you. I can't promise anything, mind you, but I did talk you up to our lighting man, Arthur Baker. He wants to talk to you first thing in the morning." And then he added, "And Nick—come prepared to work. They're hanging the next show tomorrow."

CHAPTER 18

THINGS WERE moving at warp speed. A chance to meet Arthur Baker (and to work with him, no less) and a meeting with the engineering scholarship people all in one day. So, just to be clear here, I went over my options: 1) Expose Professor Baker as a drug-dealing murderer; 2) Forget that and impress the hell out of him with my lighting abilities; 3) Blow it and wow the bio guys instead.

Life sucks sometimes, doesn't it? Dionysius.

I had used up my College Day already, so I turned on the charm with my counselor to get the day off to work at Crevette. Luckily, my counselor goes to our church, so I had her home phone number. And, even more luckily, I had taught Vacation Bible School to her five-year-old, who absolutely loved me. So I figured I had an in with his mother.

When she answered, I pled my case, skillfully omitting the unnecessary details—like my parents had no idea I was up for a theater scholarship. My skills of lying and omission had become as easy as rain rolling off a duck's back.

But, of course, she immediately countered with "Oh, Nick, your parents must be so proud of you. I *must* call your mother and offer my regards."

Think fast, think fast.

"Well, that's just it," I lied. "I haven't told my parents about the scholarship. I was hoping to surprise them." *I'm going to hell for the whoppers I've been telling.*

"Well, that's odd. I know your dad was just the other day talking to my husband, Tom, about the scholarship."

That threw me for a loop for a minute. Then I realized that she was talking about the bio money.

"Oh, that. You see, I'm also up for a scholarship at my dad's office. But—" And here I could feel hell's heat rising. "—Dad will be happy if I get either one, and you know how I love the theater." I sped up, hoping to end this call quickly. I'd thought I was comfortable with my storytelling, but she was too nice. Guilt was creeping in. "So, I need tomorrow off so I can sew this up over at the Crevette theater department and finally reveal my big surprise. I can count on you not to say anything, can't I?"

"Nick, my lips are sealed."

Bless me, Lord, for I have sinned.

I had her. And I had my extra College Day.

So—everything was all arranged. I could go to meet Baker, probe around a little, find out my killer was some other Artie Baker, amaze *this* Artie Baker with my astounding abilities, win the scholarship, tell Dad, and blow off his committee. Sweet, huh?

If only life were as easy as our fantasies. The problem came in my not being able to convince myself. My blatant untruths and inventions were weighing on me. I knew it all had to catch up with me sooner or later.

If I was going to my death—well, theater-school death, anyway— I had to see Steve first. I wanted to fill him in on what I was about to face. I suppose there was something in me that wanted him to suffer just a little of my anxiety too. I was doing this for him. Was it wrong for me to be a little selfish?

The Laughton was cold and dark that early in the morning. But as soon as the gargoyles hissed at me, Steve was there.

"Didn't expect you this early, lover," he said as he kissed me on the nose.

Then he noticed my mood. "Why so glum, chum?"

"We may solve your mystery today, babe. And in the process, seal my doom."

"What are you talking about, Nick?" There was a piercing look of concern in Steve's eyes. He really, really cared about me.

"I got a call from Nichols yesterday. You remember, the head of the theater department?"

"That's good, huh?" Steve sounded lighter, like he was hoping for good news, but his concerned look comforted me.

"Well, it could be." I took in a deep breath of the frigid Laughton air. "I'm headed over there for a sort of audition."

"Audition? What gives?" Steve took my hands. His loving touch gave me strength.

"Well, it seems that Dr. Arthur Baker, no less, wants to see me work. I'm helping them hang lights for their next show today. And if all goes well, I will have my scholarship in the bag tonight."

"That's a good thing, no?" He lit up—a grin wider than the Grand Canyon.

"Could be—yes. But then again, what if Dr. Arthur Baker is *your Artie*? Then what?"

That wiped the grin off.

"What makes you think Artie is this Dr. Baker?" Steve sounded cautious, confused.

"Because the good doctor's portrait hanging in the theater lobby looks just like the guy you described."

I swear I saw a shadow pass across Steve's face, and then a faint smile.

"Look, Nick, your future is at stake here. If *Dr.* Baker is really Artie, then so be it. But don't let exposing him destroy your chance at that scholarship. Whatever you find out today, keep it to yourself. Better yet, don't even try to find out anything."

I heard the words, but his eyes spoke far more. That look—that eternal hopelessness—washed over Steve's face.

It broke my heart.

"But if I don't find out how you died, you're trapped here forever, Steve."

"There are worse fates. Your future is what matters." Too bad Steve was a theater techie and not an actor. No matter how hard he tried, he couldn't conceal the abject loneliness he felt, trapped here in this old theater. Our brief trysts helped, but this was a soul who needed to move on.

He leaned in to hug me, but that look was still pasted on his face.

His words told me he was willing to give up eternity for me. And I believed he would do just that. But that look—it ripped me apart. And I couldn't let him make that kind of sacrifice.

It was then that I knew that I had to keep *working the case*, as they say on the cop shows. Steve needed me, and I wouldn't let him down.

I SHOWED up at the university theater at eight, ready to work as requested. There I was greeted by Susan Taylor, graduate student in theatrical lighting, as she introduced herself.

"Call me Sue, Nick—I can call you Nick, can't I?" She held out her hand for me to shake. Without waiting for the permission she had just asked for, she went on. "Nick, Dr. Baker wants us to hang lights for the upcoming show. He's inside, waiting for us, although I doubt he's standing around. That man is a powerhouse and never stops working."

It was obvious that this Sue was a total fan of Professor Arthur Baker. Would she be after I found out what I hoped to uncover?

She strode to the doors that led to the seating area, opened them, and ushered me in. I had a hard time keeping up with her as she bounded down the aisle and up the steps onto the stage.

Sure enough, Dr. Baker—I recognized him instantly—was supervising another man, who was clamping Fresnels to the first pipe.

As we approached, Baker looked over at us.

"Nick," he bellowed. He held out his hand. "I've heard so much about you. Dr. Nichols is a true champion of your ability."

I think I blushed because Sue looked at me and laughed. I took Baker's hand and shook it. His grip was strong—either the grasp of a fine, upstanding man or the grip of a maniacal assassin. I couldn't tell which. I wasn't sure I wanted to know. But I had to know. *Help me, Dionysius.*

"Let me introduce my assistant, Carl." He pointed to the other man, who looked up, saluted, and then went back to clamping the lamps on.

"Don't get too enthusiastic, Carlie," Baker said to the man. "I have to apologize for Carl here, Nick. He gets very focused when we start hanging a show."

"No prob," I said to him. Then I looked at Carl, "Great to meet you, Carl."

Carl did not respond.

"Okay, let's get started, huh?" Baker turned to Sue. "You've got the plot I gave you yesterday?"

Sue nodded.

"Fine, then. You and Nick need to go pull all the lamps we need. Carl's already pulled all the first pipe lamps."

Sue led me to a storage room. And, suddenly, life was back to normal. I was in my element. There was a familiarity here that I would guess is common to all theaters.

She consulted the plot as she directed me to the instruments that needed pulling. As we worked, we talked.

"So, why Crevette?" she asked.

"Close to home, I guess." I unclamped a Fresnel from its storage perch. "And I'm hoping to get that scholarship I heard just opened up."

"Yeah, I heard about that." She pointed to three Lekos we would need. "I would say you've got the inside track if Dr. Nichols likes you. They're moving fast on this one. The benefactor wants someone named *yesterday*, if you get my drift. They can't afford to drag their heels, I hear. If they do, he takes his money to some other school."

"Wow. Lucky for me, I'd say." What a lame-o. I was going to have to come up with more intelligent banter.

"Get one of these scoops, would you?" She pointed as she talked. She herself was pulling another scoop. "Where'd you learn about lighting?

This was something I could totally talk about. Zach was my savior.

"Well, I've done some stuff with the school drama club, but mostly, I've trained with Zach Provost at the Streetwise Players." I figured the word *trained* sounded really impressive, and tossing Zach's name around could only work in my favor. With the Players' reputation, Zach was well-known in theater circles.

"Provost, huh? Good man. Hard to believe that he is just an amateur. I've seen his work. Really solid."

"Yeah—Zach's got the chops." I kinda resented her *just an amateur* quip, but I let it go.

"What's it like, working in that creepy old Laughton? Do those gargoyles really hiss?"

I belly laughed. "You'd think they do. I swear I hear them all the time." I was not about to reveal that the Laughton was really haunted. "Seriously, though, the Laughton is pretty rundown, but it has a state-of-the-art computerized system. Amazing hardware."

"Not like the old days. Did you know that Professor Baker used to work there?"

A shiver ran up my spine. I didn't expect this. Not from her. I figured I would have to pry info out of Baker himself. Did Sue know anything about Baker's days at the Laughton that would help me?

"Really?" I played dumb.

"Sure did. Ran lights there before he finished his undergrad degree." She laughed. "A strip show, he says."

"I heard that they did burlesque there in the old days." I would take this nice and slow. Not tip my hat.

"Burlesque? Is that what they call it in the history books? To hear Dr. Baker tell it, it was just old-fashioned tits and ass."

"Well, I know one of the women who danced there, and she said it was really classy." I was getting really good at engaging conversation. Maybe I shouldn't be so hard on myself. If all this meeting new people and getting stuff out of them was any indication, I wasn't a loner. And if I could help Steve, then I guess I wasn't a loser, either.

"*Class* is in the eye of the beholder, I guess."

"Well, Layla's a very charming and refined lady, now. She claims that all the girls there were like that." I wanted to keep her talking about the Laughton. She might know something I could use.

But it was not to be.

"Let's get these to center stage," Sue ordered.

We had piled all the instruments onto a dolly, and now we guided it onto the stage.

"Here we are, Carl," Sue said. "Got everything right here."

Baker had disappeared, but Carl was still intently working.

"So start hanging," he snarled. This Carl was all work and no play, I guessed.

For about two hours, we hung lights, Sue and I keeping up a running conversation, mostly about the Crevette theater program. I never could steer her back to the stories of the old Palace. After a while, I quit trying, getting caught up in the work—and loving every minute.

Carl was as silent as a tomb.

"I got to visit the head," he announced eventually. Then he left.

Sue leaned in to me. "Carl's not much for small talk."

"What's his official position here?"

She shook her head. "Nothing."

I stared at her. Then she leaned in even closer and almost whispered. "Carl is Dr. Baker's lover."

I felt like I'd been hit with a brick. I was not expecting that. Sue chuckled at the astonished look on my face before she added, "They've been together for years and years… since high school, I've been told."

"High school?"

"Yep. The way I hear it, they fell in love and both got kicked out of their houses. Dr. Baker had gotten a work-study program, so he struggled through college and got his degree. Carl, on the other hand, had to get a job. He helped put Dr. Baker through school and never got his own degree. It's kinda sweet, if you think about it."

"Sweet?"

"Carl is totally and utterly devoted to Dr. Baker."

I wanted to know more about this Carl thing. If they had been connected at the hip that long, then Carl would know all about what went on at the Laughton. I was a little suspicious that he hadn't said anything when I was probing Sue earlier. But if he was working like we were, maybe he hadn't paid attention to what I was saying. Maybe he hadn't even heard. He was working stage left; Sue and I were stage right.

One thing was certain: Carl had to be able to tell me something. He might not know if Baker had killed Steve—that might be Baker's deep, dark secret—but Carl could tell me all I wanted to know about Baker's relationship with Vick, I would bet. Somehow, I had to talk to him.

But not then, because before I could say anything more to Sue, he and Baker appeared once more.

"You two about through here?" Baker asked.

"Just tightening the last clamp, sir," Sue answered.

"Wonderful. Looks like good work here, Nick. Any complaints about your assistant here, Sue?" He smiled at me. "Sue is my spy, Nick."

I eyed her. What a dolt I must be. Of course she was there to report on me.

"No complaints here, sir," she said. "Nick knows his stuff." Thank God she left out all the strip-show talk and kept her report strictly business.

"Wonderful," Baker exclaimed. "So, let's do some focusing. Ready for some ladder work?"

The show was a musical, so we were lighting multiple sets. Some would fly in from the rafters; others would glide in from the sides. Tough show to light, with all the changes.

"Carl, you want to join me in the booth? We'll man the board for you two."

They both disappeared as Sue and I got out the tall ladder. From the depths of the auditorium, I heard Baker's disembodied voice.

"Okay, you two. It's looking good generally. Number three, first pipe needs to be brought in to the right... a little more... more... perfect."

We continued working like that for another couple of hours; Sue or I climbing up and down the ladder and moving it when a new set piece came in.

Eventually, Baker announced, "Looks great, guys. That's the best we can do until the first tech rehearsal. Thanks, you two."

Sue gave me a high five.

From the booth, Baker, like the voice of God (or doom, as the case might be), intoned, "Sue, come up here, please." Sue immediately started for the booth. "Nick," Baker said to me, "could you just hang for a while so we can discuss your fate?"

Another chill. Zero hour. Moment of truth. Armageddon. More clichés flitted through my brain, but I'll spare you.

"Sure thing, sir," I called. "I'll just wait in the lobby."

I first made a pit stop, and then I toured the lobby, examining all the production shots that were hanging there. Next, I sat, having grabbed several brochures I'd found in a rack next to the box office. I read every single word as the time dragged on. Ask me anything about that season at Crevette University Theater, and I can tell you. The shows? The playwrights? Ticket prices? Handicapped accessible? You ask it, I can answer.

Finally, I leaned my head back against the wall, took off my glasses, blinked a few times to ease my tired eyes, and then I must have dozed off. The next thing I knew, Dr. Baker was waking me.

I looked at the clock. It was twenty minutes later than the last time I'd looked.

"Sorry to wake you, Nick." That couldn't have inspired confidence—sleeping like a baby while waiting for the biggest news of my life. Dionysius. I hoped I wasn't snoring.

I immediately stood. "I think I have good news for you," he said, smiling. "The money's yours if you still want it."

Still want it? Was he crazy? Would he think me a fool if I danced around that lobby, singing praises at the top of my lungs?

I reined in my enthusiasm and became the grateful acolyte I knew he wanted.

"Of course, I still want it, sir." I thanked him, and he explained that he would submit his approval of me to Dr. Nichols that afternoon and that Nichols would be in touch with me.

Baker must have thought I was a total idiot, because I thanked him over and over. I didn't hug him. I didn't kiss him. I didn't shake his hand off. But I couldn't stop the words. "Thank you, thank you, thank you," over and over. I think I was still thanking him even as I was clear across campus and getting into my car.

I had the scholarship. I didn't need Dad's committee. They could just take their engineering money and burn it for all I cared. The theater life was for me, and that four-year vacation was all-inclusive, thanks to this anonymous donor whose feet I would have kissed if I could.

Why is it that good feelings are fleeting?

My joy was bashed by stone-cold reality crashing in like a wrecking ball.

What if Baker—as nice as he had seemed today—was Steve's killer? After all, Sue had confirmed that Professor Arthur Baker was indeed Artie Baker, lighting guy for the Palace strippers. That meant that what Steve said about Baker being a drug dealer had to be true.

And Sue had said that Baker was strapped for money when he was in college. That could account for his dealing drugs. It didn't prove he was a killer, but it certainly pointed in that direction. I'd seen enough TV to know that drug dealing was often only the tip of the iceberg.

If I did prove that Baker had sold Vickie Stripling the drugs that killed her and Steve had somehow found out, thus necessitating Baker's murder of Steve, then it was surely bye-bye scholarship. Arthur Baker was a respected professor; he was second in command at the theater department. Would Dr. Nichols look kindly on me if I brought his friend down?

Not a chance.

I felt a headache brewing. I couldn't get those new, stronger glasses soon enough. Part of these constant headaches were tension, but seeing more clearly had to help.

This was getting to be too much for me. I had my scholarship. I could get my degree, work in the theater, and live happily ever after, instead of trying to free a trapped soul. I should just stop everything and enjoy my victory.

But Steve needed me. He deserved to know how he'd met his fate.

Shit. It looked like my fate was pretty much determined for me. I had to keep probing until I found the truth. Free Steve, then worry about my own life. If the truth sealed my doom, then so be it.

I guess I had just enough time to get home, take a shower, and put on my suit. *Engineers, I salute you.*

CHAPTER 19

THE NEXT day, as soon as I told Steve I'd gotten the theater scholarship, and before I could say anything else, he grabbed me and devoured me with hungry kisses. I have to say, those kisses pushed everything to the back of my mind. I was in heaven, and nothing else mattered right then.

We sprawled on the backstage couch, spent, just chilling, enjoying it all. I played with Steve's hair while he lay there, smiling and cooing. All the time I'd spent in my life wanting someone to love me, wishing I had a boyfriend, hoping that one special guy would come my way, and now I had him. Granted, he was a ghost, but he was mine. For that moment, life was good.

But eventually, reality crashed back in. My cell chimed, I spoke to a spaced-out ditz who had punched in the wrong number, and the moment was lost.

It was time to face what I had just avoided—quite pleasurably, I might add. But that's for some other romance novel.

"I also met with my dad's scholarship committee last night."

"Why didn't you blow them off? You got what you wanted at Crevette's theater school," Steve said. That was Steve. Maybe it was years alone trapped in a dark theater that made him so matter-of-fact. Steve was a be-yourself, take-charge-of-your-life kind of guy.

"I just couldn't." I wasn't ready to talk about Arthur Baker just yet. "Dad would have killed me if I'd left them hanging."

"So—what happened?"

"Well, they've narrowed it down to three finalists. There's me, a nerdy guy, and a girl who looks like she lives and breathes physics. I think they should give the money to her, but no one asked me."

"Why her?"

"While we were waiting for them to interview the nerd, she and I got to talking. She must not have any friends because she spilled her guts to me, a stranger. Her dad's a maintenance man at the company— barely makes minimum, she said; her mom's got MS and is bedridden. That's why she's so fired up about bioengineering. She wants to find a cure."

Sounds almost like a made-up story, but she had no reason to lie to me, and the committee would have vetted her app, so she couldn't get away with lying to them. Her story had sure got to me. If the committee felt the way I did about her, then my problem was solved.

"This would be the girl's ticket out of the life she's had, plus she might just get to help her mom to boot. And given her 190 IQ, she totally deserves to get this. Let's just hope the committee thinks so."

"How did your interview go? Were you able to steer them in that girl's direction?"

"Well…." I sighed. "I didn't get overly enthusiastic with my answers, but I couldn't deliberately blow it. Dad's boss sits on the committee, and I'd bet he gave Dad a blow-by-blow."

"So, what do you care? You've got your own scholarship all sewn up." There it was again, that you're-the-only-one-who-matters-here attitude. It did wonders for my ego, but I couldn't let myself focus totally on me and what I wanted. I loved my dad too much. What he wanted was important. Besides, there was the matter of Artie Baker, possible murderer.

"Well," I said, cautiously, "there is a slight kink in that rope."

"Huh?" Steve sat up and looked at me. "You said you got it."

"Your Artie did indeed become Dr. Arthur Baker, professor of stage lighting at Crevette University School of Theater."

"I told you to stay away from that. Your scholarship is what's important here." Could Steve be that selfless? His behavior was new to me—here I was with my dad trying to control me, and yet Steve wanted only what was best for me. I couldn't blow off this Artie Baker thing, for Steve's sake.

"We've got him. The bastard can pay now for what he did to your mom." I was resolute. No way was I going to let Steve back me away from this.

"Yes, he can," Steve said, "if you want to lose that scholarship. Come on, Nick, expose Baker as a drug dealer and possible murderer, do you think they're going to look kindly on you over there?"

I fell back into the cushions. It was all so hard. One minute, I knew I had to help Steve. Then he would bring it all back to me and my problems, and the doubt crept in. He rubbed my shoulder. It felt so good.

Could I live with myself if I did nothing, accepted the scholarship, and kept my very appealing boyfriend captive to serve my self-centered needs? Put that way, I knew what I had to do, but oh, that shoulder rub felt so wonderful.

Finally, Steve said, "Keep quiet. That's the only thing to do. You clam up, and the scholarship stays yours."

Those were his words, but I was hearing something entirely different, deep down, below the surface. Steve wanted to be supportive. That's the kind of guy he was. But underlying it all, he was trapped for eternity. He knew it, and I knew it.

"Do you really want me to do that?" I asked.

"Of course I do. I love you, Nick. This is your life we're talking about here."

But he was trying too, too hard to convince me. And himself.

"And what about you?" I probed.

"What *about* me?" A tremble in his voice.

"Stevie...." I kissed his earlobe. I thought I was trying to put him at ease so he would admit the truth. Instead, I realize I was probably trying to convince him that staying with me wasn't a good move. My next words were designed to convince him that he needed release; they could have also been a seductive promise.

"You'll never, ever leave here."

"But I'll have you. That's all I need." He wanted to convince himself. I heard it.

The tiny catch in his voice, the barely discernible doubt, convinced me of what I must do. I could not let him remain in limbo, no matter how much doing so might serve my needs.

"Really? Did you have me the first twenty years you were here? How was that working for you, as Dr. Phil would say?"

"Dr. Phil? Who's that?"

"My point exactly. You're stuck here. No contact with the outside world, except for me. Well, what happens when life happens? Say I get this great job on the road? I can't take you with me. Then what?"

I bombarded him with reality.

"It's okay. I'll wait for you."

I needed to keep pushing buttons.

"And, say, forty years from now. You'll still be this teenage hunk. Are you going to want to make it with an old man? 'Cause that's who I'll be."

"I'll always love you, Nick." His words spoke truth, but they sounded like he might be caving. It was time to drop the bomb.

"And I can't live forever. You can't count on my getting stuck here like you. I'll be gone. How will you handle that?"

"I can do it, Nick. I'll have my memories." The way he said *memories,* I knew I was being cruel to get him to understand and accept. It was working.

I kept pounding away.

"Memories? Will those keep you going for the next fifty years? A hundred years? Two hundred?"

"Stop it, Nick." Steve held his head with both his hands, like he was trying to squeeze from it the image I'd conjured. I knew I almost had him ready to accept that my potentially sacrificing the scholarship was what needed to happen. Still, he tried to convince himself: "I'll manage."

"Well, I can't live with it. I can't deal with knowing I'm standing between you and heaven or nirvana or release or whatever the hell we want to call it. I can't do that to you, Stevie. I love you too much to make you suffer like that."

I pulled him to me and held him. We were both sobbing by then. Tears of release. Tears of loss.

Then, I felt in my heart more than heard him say: "I'm afraid. Afraid of an empty existence like I had before you, Nick."

I clasped his head to my heart.

"Don't worry, Stevie. I'm going to take care of it."

CHAPTER 20

FIRST THINGS first—I had to find out everything I could about Artie Baker. Thank Dionysius for cyberspace. After googling his name, I felt like an expert about Professor Arthur Baker... award-winner, published author, successful teacher. But curse the limitations of cyberspace: sometimes the supposedly insignificant things fall through the cracks. That part of his life when he was just plain Artie was a blank.

I had to know more. It was time for old-fashioned sleuthing.

Who might be able to fill me in? I asked myself the question when I already knew the answer.

Well, she had told me to come again sometime, so I decided it was time to pay Layla another visit.

Layla seemed really happy to get my call. She invited me to tea that very next day. Tea? I've seen tea parties in movies. Didn't seem like anything I'd ever get an invite for. But my life had never included anyone like Layla before, with her vast wealth and huge servant-filled mansion. Still, can you imagine? Sitting down to my first tea with a former stripper?

But Layla was more than that—besides being that infinitely wealthy grande dame, she was a genuinely likeable person. And there's where my seeing her again got tricky. And guilt inducing. I hated lying to her, but I had to know what she knew.

Billy the butler greeted me at the door, after the guard at the gate had motioned me through. I was shown into the drawing room, where

Layla sat in state, like she was awaiting the queen's arrival—or was the regal one herself.

When she saw me, though, all that pretense melted away. She jumped up and ran to me, grabbing me in a big bear hug. Layla was one of kind, believe you me.

"Nicky, I'm so happy you came to see little ol' me. This ol' lady doesn't get many visitors these days, especially young hunks like you." Carried herself like Gran; flirted like the former stripper she was. I loved her.

I kissed her on the cheek. "Now, Layla," I flirted back, "I'd bet you have to beat off young men with a stick."

I've learned a lot about handling older women with my Gran. They love to think that they are still sexual beings. Don't we all like to think of ourselves that way?

My comment got a schoolgirl giggle out of Layla.

"Come, come," she said, coyly. "Sit yourself down, and tell me what's happenin' in your life. I can't tell you how happy you've made me, comin' to see me again like this."

She sat and poured cups of tea for us both, humming a tune the whole time.

"One lump or two?" she asked, holding little silver tongs over a sugar bowl, continuing her happy song.

"Three, please," I answered, remembering Layla's sweet tooth.

"My, my, my… we do have a sweet tooth. I like that in my young men. Here we go." She put three sugars in my cup. "Sweets for the sweet." She handed me my cup, then burst into full-blown song.

"Layla, you are something else," I said, taking the cup from her. "What is that melody I hear?" I smiled slyly, pretending that she wasn't singing at the top of her lungs.

She giggled. "That, my deah, is a little ditty I used in my act. I've always been in love with love. And my signature song was that tune, 'Love Makes the World Go 'Round.'" She sang some more of it, this time using the words and not just the *la-la-la*s she'd sung before.

"Pretty song, Layla. Sung by a pretty lady." You'd think I was laying it on thick for my own purposes, but I meant every word.

Layla's glowing beauty showed right through any aging her body had been through. "I know you wowed 'em when you were dancing."

Another giggle, accompanied by a gesture that said *you flatter me*. It was obvious, though, that she liked being flattered.

"Enough about me, sugar. Fill me in. What's goin' on with you?"

She somehow kept her eyes and attention on me as she served me one of the little cakes we both had adored at our last meeting.

"Thanks," I said, setting the plate down and continuing. "Well, I got a scholarship this week." I made it sound like it was nothing so that, hopefully, she would ask more questions. I even paused to take a bite of cake. I was back in my omission/lying mode, hating every minute of deceiving Layla but knowing it was necessary. *Forgive me, Dionysius.*

"Scholarship? Darlin', tell old Layla all about it." She was just like Gran—ever interested in each little morsel of my life.

"Well, I applied at the Crevette University School of Theater and found out this week that I got it."

"Fantastic, my little love. What subject?"

"Theatrical lighting."

"What? Have you been holdin' out on me? I didn't know you were interested in the theater. You didn't mention that at all when we met before."

Didn't have time, I thought. *Too busy pumping you for info.* Oh, the tangled webs we weave....

"I didn't? I can't believe it. Usually, you can't shut me up about it. I guess I was too focused on my project then."

"What's your background, darlin'? Just because Layla *danced* for a living doesn't mean that she doesn't appreciate the legitimate theater. If you're good enough to get a scholarship, then you must have done some serious trainin'."

She took a piece of cake for herself, saying, "You need more, honey?"

I pointed to my plate. "Still got some, but you can bet I'll want seconds when I finish this." *If I'm still welcome here.*

"You can have all you want, sugar. Now go on. Layla wants to hear all about this."

"I volunteer with the Streetwise Players," I said.

"At my old stompin' ground, the Palace?"

"Well, they call it the old name, the Laughton, but yeah, I work there. Anyway, Zach Provost, their lighting man, is one of the very best. He's taught me a ton of things."

"I can't believe you never mentioned that you worked at the same theater where I danced. Why were ya holdin' out on me? Was it some deep dark secret, darlin'?"

"No, Layla, I swear." I had to charm away my blunder. Layla was too smart not to at least think about why I'd never mentioned my working at the Laughton when I supposedly had come before to talk about the theater. What was I thinking of? I wasn't as good at deception then. I was only thinking of getting information and not covering my tracks. "I got so caught up in your tales of the old Palace that I just never got around to talking about me. You're a charmer, Layla." I smiled at her. "Just like a snake charmer with his cobra, you had me in a trance, just wanting to hear more of your fascinating life."

Pul-leeze. I didn't believe me; why should she? I guess I still wasn't as good at wool-over-eyes-pulling as I thought I was.

But Layla bought it, hook, line, and sinker. And I was beginning to feel the guilt wash over me for how I was manipulating her.

"Well, Nicky, I am pleased as punch that you are *in the theater,* as we say. I knew you and I had a connection the moment we met. I could just feel it."

"Layla, you are so sweet," I gushed. Bullet dodged.

"So, tell me more about this scholarship, dearie."

"It's a full ride: tuition, books, housing, plus spending money. I couldn't ask for anything better. And—" Now it was time to bait the hook. "—I'll be working with one of the country's best lighting guys, Arthur Baker."

Her smile vanished; Layla's face turned dark. A memory had just settled a black cloud right over her head, I was sure.

"What? What is it, Layla? Why so glum, chum?" I used Steve's favorite phrase without thinking.

"What did you say?"

"I asked why you look so unhappy all of a sudden," I said, purposely avoiding repeating Steve's words.

"That expression you used, though. It was Vick's." I saw a tear fall from Layla's eye. Then she sat up straighter, fighting to stay in control. My heart was breaking. I'd come to this lovely lady's house, accepted her graciousness, played her like a fiddle, and now pulled something so dark from her that it instantly plunged her into despair. I was a shit.

But Layla was a survivor. "Remember I told you about her? You just brought her back to me…." I saw the struggle. She fought to keep herself together.

Then she started sobbing.

I put my hand on her arm. I felt helpless. I cursed myself for causing this despair in her. "Whatever is bothering you, Layla, it's okay," I said, trying to comfort her and feeling like I was not doing a very good job of it.

This was getting to be too much for me to handle. I'd come there for information, not to destroy an old woman.

Almost as quickly as the crying started, it stopped. Layla grabbed a napkin off the tea tray and dabbed at her eyes. "No. No, no, no, no. I will not do this. That was ages ago. It's just water under the bridge. I'm not gonna bawl my eyes out jus' 'cause you used Vick's favorite expression."

I had come there to do a job. I was heartbroken that I'd done this to her. I would be a royal asshole if I caused her any more pain. I took a deep breath and twisted the knife.

"But you were upset before I said that." If—*big if*—I could help Steve, then this was worth it. How easy it is to convince ourselves when love is involved. Not my love for Steve, but his love for me. He was willing to sacrifice himself for me. I could do the same, even if it meant being a shit with an old lady who graced the earth, not hurting anyone.

"You're right, sugar." She sighed. "It was that name you mentioned. Arthur Baker? Only I knew him as Artie Baker, a green li'l ol' college kid who did some bad things."

"Like what?" I probed. Prodded.

"No. What Artie Baker did can't be undone, so we might as well just let it lay."

I'd come too far to turn back. I could not let her stop now. No matter what the cost.

"Don't do this to me, Layla, please." I searched my brain for an argument she'd buy. It came to me when I realized she really cared about me. Again, the cost. The cost of using this wonderful lady. I made it all about me.

"If I'm going to be working with the guy at the university, I need to know what you're talking about."

Her manner changed. I had her. Her concern for me convinced her to spill the dope. And I wanted to crawl into a hole for how I was using her. I was going to have a take a long, hot shower to wash away this crap I was traipsing in.

"He was just little Artie when we knew him: dear, sweet Artie. But he's the one who got Vick hooked again. He brought that vile stuff into the theater, and poor Vick was weak enough to succumb." The memory didn't destroy her again. The anger it brought back made her stronger. She drew herself up, looking very determined to face it.

"Layla, are you telling me that Dr. Baker is a drug dealer?"

"Was, Nick, *was*…. I'm sure now he is a very respectable member of the community. He was a youngster back in those days, still in college. I forgave him a long, long time ago." I could believe that. I could also believe that *forgive* didn't equal *forget*. "I'm just a sentimental ol' lady, tearing up just hearing his name. It wasn't his fault, really. We were all just trying to make a buck. I don't think Artie ever realized what he was doing to poor Vick. And believe you me, she had me fooled as well. I had no idea she was indulgin' in Artie's wares. I would have done anything in my power to stop that. She was so vulnerable."

"So he dealt the drugs that killed her?"

"Not directly."

What? *Not directly?* What was she saying? I was convinced that Baker was a drug dealer, and she was saying otherwise. My heart fell. If Baker wasn't responsible for Vick's death—and Steve's—then I was up another blind alley.

"Oh, Artie dealt a little grass. Seemed like *everybody* did in those days, when they was short of money. And he did sell to Vick. What he couldn't have known was that Vick was a recovering addict. She couldn't stop with just a little weed, like the rest of us gals. She got in deeper and deeper and deeper. And I guess we were all just young and stupid enough to think that what we were doing ourselves had nothin' to do with Vick and that she wasn't goin' to buy from Artie. No, Artie didn't kill Vick; he just started the downward spiral."

"So she bought the drugs that killed her somewhere else?" I wanted to scream. Baker was not my killer. Layla was proving that and plunging me back into that hole, this time for a different reason.

"Yeah… she never said where. That was something we didn't talk about. I guess she had a street dealer."

"So you're saying that you don't blame Dr. Baker for your friend's death?" I was clutching at anything, trying to pull myself out of the abyss.

"No, Artie was a real dear. We all loved him. And talent… that boy could do things with our old lighting system that you wouldn't believe. It's no wonder he's where he is now." She paused. I could see good memories flying across her brain. Any dark thoughts she may have had of Baker had dissipated. "No, Artie was a sugar pie. Now, that boyfriend of his, he was a horse of a different color." Her voice turned dark once again.

"Boyfriend?"

"What was his name? Marley? Charlie? Merle?" She wracked her brain. "No. Wait. It was Carl. That was his name. And he was a surly kid. I never knew what Artie saw in him."

"Carl, you say? I met him the other day when I met Dr. Baker."

"They're still together? After all these years? I had hoped poor Artie would finally rid himself of that little pissant."

"Carl seemed okay to me. He is totally devoted to Dr. Baker, or so I'm told."

"Oh, that's half the problem. He stuck to Artie like a fly to flypaper. He was always around. And God forbid, if you said anything at all cross to Artie. That little bastard—'scuse my French, dear—was always there to defend him. No, Artie would have been better off getting rid of Carl years ago."

CHAPTER 21

Layla didn't have any more details. She didn't like Carl, and that was that. She couldn't say exactly why except that she thought he wasn't good enough for Baker, and I couldn't drag anything else out of her. I didn't know if I'd learned anything useful from Layla or not. I would lay it all before Steve and hear what memories floated up from his dead brain.

When I left Layla's, I checked my cell. I had planned to head straight for the Laughton, but Wash had left me a text message saying my glasses were ready for pickup. So I stopped by there first.

As the sliding doors whooshed open in front of me, a huge smile flashed across Wash's face. He held up a small bundle.

"I've been waiting for you. Your new specs are right here." And he again held up the bundle, which I now could see was a case with a receipt rubber-banded around it. The smile he wore seemed more than the smile of a grateful salesman. I quickly dismissed that notion.

Wash's greeting, however, was enough to make me forget the Steve/Artie situation for a few blissful minutes. I had forgotten how much I liked the guy. My *nether* region hadn't forgotten, however.

When he motioned for me to sit, I did so very quickly, needing to hide that little somethin' somethin' growing in my pants. Luckily, he didn't seem to notice.

He snapped the rubber band and took out the glasses.

"These are beautiful, Nick. You're going to love them," he said. "It will just take a minute to fit them."

He made some adjustments before he placed them on my nose. His hand brushed against my cheek, and I shivered. Wash was the first real guy who had ever touched my face, and, even though he was just doing his job, it felt good.

Now, at this point, you're asking, "What about Steve?" *Pause.* Has it sunk in yet? Yes, Steve had touched me, and yes, it felt wonderful, but... *okay*—now you've got the picture. Steve wasn't flesh and blood, right? Steve turned me on faster that I'd ever thought possible, but there was something more *complete* about what I felt right then with Wash.

I felt a little pulse, a little throb, as Wash's warm breath blew across my forehead while he checked the fit of those glasses.

"There. Perfecto." As he turned the mirror toward me, he snickered, cautioning, "Careful. Images in the mirror may be too intense for casual glances. You're smokin', Nick."

Was this guy a good salesman or what? I knew he had to say things like that to all his customers, but he was very convincing. He knew his business. Make 'em feel like they're super special and they'll be back for more. God knows, I wanted to buy a pair a week if this was the kind of service I'd get.

"They *do* look good, don't they?" I said to him. Then I looked into the distance. "And Doc was right: things are a lot clearer with these."

"We amped up the lenses a lot. 'Clearer' should be an understatement." Wash handed me the case for them. "If you have any problems, I'm here for you." He smiled. He offered his hand for me to shake, concluding our business.

I took it in mine. The handshake seemed to last a little longer than most. But that was my growing desire talking, I told myself.

I carefully hung the jacket I was carrying in front of me so that my hard-on wouldn't be so noticeable as I stood.

"Thanks, Wash. See you around."

In the car, I stared into the rearview. I really did look hot, if I must say so. I couldn't believe that new glasses could make such a difference. If you got to wear 'em, then you need someone like Wash to help you pick 'em out. End of commercial.

I couldn't wait for Steve to see me; I was that excited.

He greeted me like usual when I stepped through the stage door, grabbing me, tonguing me... well, you get the picture. He had me so turned on that I almost forgot where I was, what I'd done that day, and what I needed to talk to him about. Now I really was confused. Just a short time ago, I was thinking that Wash was the real thing and Steve was just an illusion. Then I walked in here, and Steve had me so worked up that I was not thinking straight at all.

After he finally calmed down so we could talk (and I cooled off a bit), my mind focused.

"I saw Layla this afternoon," I told him.

His face brightened. "How's she doing?" he asked.

"Same old Layla. She's a hoot and a half, as my gran says." We sat on the couch. He rubbed my leg, but I was determined to ignore his advances and stay on topic. I was a man with a mission.

"Do you remember a guy named Carl?" I began slowly, hoping to pull something new out of Steve.

"Carl? Sure—he was attached to Artie's right hip. But he didn't have much to do with anything here: hung a few lights, sometimes worked the board."

"Anything else you remember?"

"Yeah, Carl was a real creep. He threw off bad vibes. He got super worked up if anybody said anything bad to Artie."

"Bad? Like what?" What Layla couldn't pinpoint, maybe Steve could.

"Nothing really. The girls were always joking around, calling people names. Layla was the worst. She loved to call people *pissants*. It was a Southern thing. She could call Carl that, and he wouldn't even blink, but when she used it on Artie, Carl was all over her."

So that's why Layla didn't like him. She must have blocked that particular memory—or she didn't think it important enough to share with me.

As Steve talked, I stared into his eyes, searching for something, anything, a clue, a hint of an answer. Something to nail Carl to the wall.

His not liking Layla didn't label him a murderer. If not Carl, maybe this new bout of reminiscence would reveal something.

Nothing had panned out so far. Layla certainly didn't kill Steve. Trey's life had turned out better because of Steve. He hadn't known that at the time, but deep down, he must have realized that he was going to have to cut ties with Daddy sooner or later, and Steve had started the long process. So I was convinced that George Mervyn III was not our killer. Bert had ruled himself *and* the boss out. And I, for very personal and selfish reasons, didn't want to believe that Professor Baker had killed Steve. Carl was the only one left.

Dionysius, a light switched on over my head. A revelation. A clarity that I'd never had before. I could see it all, just as it was happening.

I paced the stage and shouted questions at Steve. "What kind of dealings did you have with Carl?" I was so excited at my vision of it all that I was barking.

Steve's brow wrinkled. Maybe my agitation was scaring him, but I knew I had the answer.

"Not much—that I can remember. He mostly just sat around and waited for Artie."

I couldn't stop now. I knew I was on to something; it was crystal clear. "Do you remember anything more about what happened after you confronted Artie?" I demanded, trying to draw a new memory out of him. "Maybe Artie did something. Maybe he wasn't telling you the truth that night. Maybe he waited for you after you thought it was all over." Everything poured out of me, one thought following another. "Think, Steve. You've remembered everything else that happened that night. You can remember this if you try."

There was a long, long pause, during which I picked up my pacing. Steve had to confirm this movie that was playing in my head.

Steve stood, his eyes widening.

"What, Steve? What are you seeing?" I had the picture. He had to have it too. And it had to be as clear and perfect as mine was. "What happened that night? You remember something else, don't you?"

"It's all coming back now. I confronted Artie." It was Steve's turn to pace. I needed him to replay that scene until it merged with the scene I was envisioning. "He swore that he didn't sell Mama the drugs—

those drugs that killed her. He admitted that he had sold her some pot, but that was all. I wanted to slam him up against a wall, but suddenly, he started crying. 'I didn't know she had a problem, Stevie,' he blubbered. 'I never would have done anything to Vick on purpose. She was always nice to me. I feel so bad for what happened. Vick didn't deserve what happened to her. It was my fault, Stevie, my fault. I'm so, so sorry.' And before I knew it, he was grabbing me, hugging me, crying buckets on my shoulder."

Steve took two steps toward me, visibly shaken. It was wishful thinking, but I thought I saw the movie playing on his retinas.

"Nick, it wasn't Artie. Artie said he had some big paper due. He left after the show started—after we talked. I think he was so shook up that he just wanted to get out of there. He left Carl to run the show for him."

Bingo—the images, in glorious Technicolor, IMAX, 3D, were coming together, pointing toward the climax we'd been searching for.

"Okay. Great. Keep it coming, Steve. Did Carl do anything to you? Tell me, buddy. It's right there, waiting to come out." I pointed to his brain cavity, punctuating each word.

And then Steve staggered back. He collapsed on the sofa. It was like a wave of nausea washed over him.

"Carl left as soon as the final show was over. I stuck around, helping the girls cart their stuff. By the time I got to the dressing rooms, Layla had already gone. The girls said *her Sam*, as she called him, had taken her out of there as soon as the show was over. The other girls had years of junk to clear out. And they were all in tears, with the theater closing and all."

Steve was hugging himself, lost in the memory. It broke my heart, but my heart had broken several times that day. This was a necessary damage.

"Finally, after the girls had all left, I locked the front door and headed out the back, into the parking lot. There were only two cars left. Mine was sitting over in the corner where I'd left it. The other car? It was Carl's, headlights on, waiting."

Steve held up his hand, like he was shielding his eyes.

"Suddenly, I heard Carl gun his engine. The car was coming right at me, like he was aiming for me. It was happening so fast that I didn't even have time to scream." Steve was balled up on the couch now, as if his whole body was in pain. "The weight was unbearable. Pressing on me. Squeezing the life out of me." Steve was gasping for breath. "I tried to breathe. I could only feel tiny little gasps. Nothing was entering my lungs. Then the tires backed up. But I still couldn't breathe. I couldn't keep my eyes open. Through slits, I saw Carl, hovering over me."

Steve winced, agonizing with every memory of that night. I almost stopped him. It was too much to bear, for me. But I had to bear it, for Stevie.

"I was trying to breathe, trying to cling to something, a thought, a feeling, anything that would tell me I was still alive. But it was over. The last thing—and this is really the last thing—I remember is Carl dragging me. After that, nothing. That had to be the moment when I died, Nick."

And just like a baby in his mother's womb, Steve was balled up on the couch in the fetal position, back in the only safe place he'd ever known.

And the weirdest thing had happened—I didn't notice until Steve was there, exhausted from the memories: Steve seemed to be fading, little by little. My ghost boyfriend was regaining his memories and, in the process, starting to reclaim himself.

I slipped down onto the sofa, caressing Steve, trying desperately to comfort him. I wanted to tell him that I was certain now that if we could pin it all on Carl, if we could make him confess, then Steve would be released, that he could go home to his mom finally.

But Steve was not in any state to hear what I would say. At that moment, I felt totally helpless.

The quiet was deafening. Even the gargoyles were silent. My heart was breaking for Steve. I had pushed and pushed until there was nothing left for him to cling to... his memory loss was the only thing that had kept him going all these years.

But if my theory was right, all this was a good thing for him. I had to make him understand. He seemed so lost right then.

Steve reached up and ran his fingers across my cheek. Then he pulled me down toward him.

This was agonizing. I had destroyed him. He had been happier not knowing what had happened to him. I had to make it right.

His lips gently met mine.

"Thank you, Nick," he whispered. His arms circled me. "You freed me."

Steve *did* understand it all. He *knew* he had to remember in order to continue his journey to wherever we go eventually.

"No, Steve," I said, "you freed yourself. But you're still here. Here in this theater. And I think I know why. I think I've always known why. Your soul or spirit or whatever is trapped here for a reason.

"You never left here. This is where you died. Carl had to have dragged your body back into the theater, and this is where Carl must have stashed your body."

"Stashed my body? Where?"

"Could be anywhere in this old place. There are nooks and crannies that nobody's been in for years and years."

"So you think my bones are locked away someplace, right here where we could find them?"

"Right here, Stevie. Uneasily resting with the gargoyles. This damp old cavern has become a holding cell. A *Steve's spirit* holding cell."

A holding cell for ghosts? Steve looked at me like I had just pronounced his eternal damnation.

"There's great news in all this, Steve," I said, trying desperately to comfort him. "It sounds crazy, but while you were just having that meltdown, I saw you fading, like the memories were trying to free you. I *know* that we are on the right track now.

"Carl must have stashed your body somewhere in here," I continued, "and you can't leave it for some reason. I think somehow your spirit has unfinished business."

"Unfinished business?"

"You can't leave without catching Carl—if he did this. And I'm certain he did."

He kissed me again. "Nick, you're a genius." Then he sighed. "But how do we nail Carl?"

"Well, I can't just go to the police. Even if they already knew about your death, they wouldn't have any reason to pick up the guy."

"So we've got to lure him here and somehow get him to confess."

"Easier said than done, chum."

"You could call him and ask him to meet you here," Steve said.

"Right: 'Carl, could you come over to the Laughton so I can accuse you of murdering my ghostly boyfriend?' That ought to get him here pronto."

"Well, think of something else, then." Steve bit his lip, obviously thinking. "What about...." And then he was silent. "How about...." He tried again, but immediately said, "No, that wouldn't work, either."

I felt for the guy. Here we were, close to solving this mess, and we were stuck. I looked around at the old theater, staring at the gargoyles, the silent witnesses to Steve's death, begging for their help.

And it was like they hissed the answer right at me.

"This place is in serious need of repair, right?" I said.

"Yeah," Steve nodded, his eyes all scrunched up, trying to figure my angle.

"And the Streetwise Players has a lot of rich benefactors."

"Where you going with this, Nick?"

"Stay with me here." I put my fingers on his lips, hushing him. "Suppose I go to Dr. Baker's house, wait until he leaves, then talk to Carl. I'll tell him that the Laughton Theater is getting a complete makeover and suggest he and Dr. Baker come over for a last look before the place is gutted. I could make it sound like a trip down memory lane for them."

"Uh-huh." Steve was finally getting my drift.

"If I'm right about Carl's stashing your body here somewhere, then he'll need to get rid of it before the 'construction crew' comes in."

"And we'll be here when he shows up."

"Right. I'll offer to open up for him, and then I'll make myself scarce. Hopefully, we'll catch him in the act."

"Nick, this will work—I know it will." He planted a big, sloppy kiss on me.

"Don't get too excited, Stevie. We could be way off base with this Carl thing." I saw his face fall. "But I don't think so."

So we had a plan. A plan that would whisk Steve's spirit away—just like our special effect. And I never once stopped to think of the consequences for me. I was so happy that Steve would be at peace that the thought of losing my first boyfriend never entered my mind. Maybe that's what love is.

After I left the theater and was in the car planning my *invitation* for Carl, I realized something: Steve had never even noticed my new glasses.

CHAPTER 22

CARL WAS waiting for me at the stage door when I pulled up the next afternoon. That morning, I had stopped by Dr. Baker's house on my way into school. Well, actually, I had staked the place out, waiting for Baker to leave. I knew he had an early class that morning, and I was hoping that Carl wasn't so glued to him that he would go in with him.

Sure enough, Baker left the house alone right on cue.

I rang the doorbell, and Carl answered. He stood in the doorway, not looking happy to see me. "What do you want?" he asked. "Dr. Baker's already left. And he's not in the habit of seeing students in his home, anyway."

"That's okay, Carl." I used his name on purpose, hoping to sound friendlier. All part of the plan. "I just have a message for him—and you too, I suppose."

"Haven't you heard of telephones?" He started to shut the door.

Jerk. But then I smiled, turning on the charm so I could win him over to my side.

"Wait." I held up my hand. "I had this idea after I left home this morning. And wouldn't you know it? My cell's dead. Since you're on my way to school, I decided to just stop by."

"Huh," he snorted. The murdering shit.

I stayed on track.

"Look, I just thought you'd like to know something, that's all. You know how I work at the Streetwise Players?"

He nodded, that sneer a permanent scar across his face.

"Well, I was visiting my friend Layla Burns yesterday...." I looked for some recognition, but Carl was stone-faced, so I notched up my charm a few degrees more. "She told me how Artie—as she called Dr. Baker—used to do lights at the old Laughton when she worked there."

"Must have been somebody else," he said, stepping back and starting again to shut the door. He really was a nasty person. Of course, I guess most cold-blooded killers are.

"Look, Carl, I know Layla was a stripper. And I also know that a strip show is not the most advantageous line item on Dr. Baker's resume. But when he worked at the Laughton, Layla's show was a lot classier than the tit shows today. She told me how it was almost a family there, and how you and Dr. Baker were part of that family."

What was with the tiny smile that crossed his face? Was there a heart locked in his homicidal body?

"You guys were young then." I continued piling it on. The deeper the manure, the more mired in it he'd become. "Dr. Baker was getting valuable experience for the fantastic career he's had." Praising the love of his life—the love he'd killed for. That would butter him up. "And believe me, if that's a part of Dr. Baker's life he wants to keep quiet, then I'll never mention it to anyone."

"So why are you here? Nick, isn't it?" He seemed to be softening up. But I wasn't fooled. This guy was a cold-blooded sociopath.

"Here's the deal.... Streetwise has gotten this huge grant for renovation. They're bringing in a crew in a few days to completely gut the theater. Everything will be new. There's even talk of getting rid of the gargoyles. I think that's a mistake, but they haven't asked me."

When I mentioned the gargoyles, a smile crossed his face. What was up with that?

"So," I continued, "I thought that you and Dr. Baker might like to see the old place one last time before everything starts happening. That's why I saw Layla yesterday," I lied, "so she could tour the Palace, as she calls it. It brought back a ton of memories for her. And she told me, 'Nick, I wish the girls and everybody else could see this place again. They'd really have a great time.' She kept thanking me and thanking me. You know how Layla is.

"So when I asked her if she thought Dr. Baker would like a tour, she insisted that I ask you guys.

"I have a key and I could get you in—this afternoon if you want, after I'm done with school." I had baited the hook; now I needed to reel him in.

"It's just a thought I had. If you and Dr. Baker can't make it, it's no biggie." I turned, like I was leaving.

"Wait, Nick," I heard Carl say. I turned around. The man was all smiles. I had him.

"The Palace was a great place to work," he relented—for nefarious reasons, I was sure. "And I *would* like to see it again. Arthur is in class all day, then rehearsal later. But if you're willing, I would like to come. Seeing the old place will bring back some really good memories."

How could he say that with a straight face? Or was offing Steve a good memory for him?

"Great, Carl. I can meet you at four o'clock." I would concoct some story to leave him alone in the theater later. I wanted to hide and see what he would do.

"I'll be there," he said, that smile still plastered on his face.

As I turned to leave, his voice stopped me.

"You know, Nick," he said, "I know that old place like the back of my hand. If you've got anything else you need to do this afternoon, you could just let me in to wander around, and then you could come back later. I don't want to get you in any trouble, leaving a stranger there, but sometimes memories are best experienced in solitude."

So much for me needing a reason to leave. He was making my job a lot easier.

"Carl," I said, trying to ooze congeniality, "you're no stranger to the Laughton. As a matter of fact, I cleared your visit with the Streetwise president already"—I lied—"and she's cool with the idea. She told me any time you and Dr. Baker wanted to come was okay. I know she won't mind at all if it's just you."

I felt warm inside, proud of this major whopper I'd just told. My mom would be horrified that I had become such a perfect prevaricator.

"Well, that's just great, Nick. I'm looking forward to spending some time with the gargoyles," he laughed, a tiny little, almost insidious laugh. "Sounds funny, but I used to talk to 'em."

Doesn't sound funny at all, Carl. You're crazy as a loon. "I know exactly what you mean, Carl. I have had some conversations with them myself."

Carl smiled again. I was feeling like Sherlock Holmes, Hercule Poirot, Lieutenant Columbo, and the *Law & Order* squad all put together. I'd laid my trap, and Carl was walking right into it.

"As luck would have it," I told him, "I do have an errand to run this afternoon for Zach—he's the lighting director, you know. It would save me a lot of my afternoon if I just opened up, let you in to wax nostalgically while I go on my run. It should take me about an hour and half. Will that give you enough time in the old place?"

He had set this up perfectly for me. If he thought I wouldn't be there, he could do whatever he wanted, and that, I hoped, would lead to Steve's release.

"Sure, Nick, that will be plenty of time. I just want to see the old place, say good-bye to the 'goyles." He laughed.

The dung was getting very deep. Carl was trying very hard to make me think he was a normal guy with normal feelings.

We agreed on a time, and that's when I met Carl at the stage door.

"Wow, you're early," I called to him as I got out of my car.

"I just wanted to sit in the old parking lot a minute alone," he said.

Why? So you could relive Steve's murder? I thought.

But Carl was all smiles. Dammit, the guy could turn it on when he wanted. He was playing this act to the hilt. I saw right through him, but he was trying to be Mr. Congeniality. I had to give him credit.

I put in my key and opened the door. "Step right in," I said, as I motioned him to enter before me.

I flipped the work lights on. True to form for that old building, the light right above the door there flickered on, then burned out, leaving us in semidarkness. I pushed Carl toward the stage, where there was light. Then, I looked around for Steve. He was never around when anyone else but me was there, but I knew he would come out for this.

"Old place look any different?" I said.

"Pretty much the same," Carl said as he strolled around the stage.

I spied Steve standing in the wings across from Carl.

"Layla tells me that the girls painted the gargoyles."

Carl laughed. "Yeah, I remember when they did that. Said the old 'goyles freaked 'em out."

I stood silently as Carl gazed at the multicolored wall monsters. It seemed he really was moved, being here. Damn, damn, damn, damn, damn. Could Steve's memory have been wrong? Was Carl really a cold-hearted killer? Or was Steve's death an accident? *Don't doubt yourself now, Nick. He's the one. You know it. It's as clear as day.*

"Look," I said, "I can see that you are having some flashbacks here. And you don't need me here to lead you down memory lane. Like I said this morning, Zach does have that job for me. Luckily, the place I need to go to is not far from here. On a gorgeous day like today, I think I'll walk. So I'll get out of your hair. Have fun. See you in an hour, hour and a half at the most."

"Thanks, Nick, but I won't need nearly that long. I just want to take a quick good-bye tour. Tell you what, you lock up the back door and when I'm finished, I'll just leave through the front doors. They used to lock behind you. They still do that?"

"Yep, they do," I answered, thinking, *So it won't take long for you to dispose of Steve's bones, huh?*

"Well, then, you just run along. Enjoy the sunshine. I'm feeling at home again here," he said.

I left Carl center stage, went over to the stage door and locked it, then jogged up the aisle to the lobby. There, I opened the one door in the bank of four that I knew squeaked something fierce. Looking cautiously over my shoulder, I shut it, so Carl would think I was gone. Then I snuck back into backstage by way of the side door.

Steve turned when he felt me standing by him. "You think we have him?" he asked, pointing across the stage to Carl.

"I don't know, Stevie," I whispered. "So far, he's not looking like a killer. Let's just watch and see." I didn't want to get Steve's hopes up.

Carl wandered around the stage, looking up into the fly space. Then he stared out into the seating area. "Still hissing, guys?" he said out loud.

"Who's he talking to?" Steve asked.

"The gargoyles," I answered, shaking my head.

"Still see everything?" Carl asked, still gazing at the wall monsters. "It's a good thing all you can do is hiss," he said. "Hiss-ss-ss-sss-ssss...." There was a grotesque smile on his face.

And then he turned. Slowly and deliberately, he walked toward the old lighting control box.

"Why's he going there?" Steve said. "That thing hasn't been opened since they put in the new system. Do you think that's where he stashed my body?"

"Could be," I whispered.

"But wouldn't I have started to stink?"

I looked at Steve. "When everyone left the theater that night, it was locked up. The Laughton just sat here, empty, remember? By the time Streetwise got interested in the old place, the smell would have been long gone."

Carl looked ghostly standing there, the light spill from the stage dimly lighting him.

I whipped out my cell to capture video of what was happening. The day before, I had tried my phone camera in all sorts of light just to make sure it would work. I couldn't take any chances. That video was going to put Carl away for life.

And that would mean Steve's freedom.

Carl took something from his pocket. A black plastic garbage bag billowed as he snapped it open. He looked around constantly, probably watching for my return, as he worked quickly.

"What's he doing?" Steve asked. I was startled by Steve's voice, fearing Carl would hear him. Then I remembered that I was the only one who could see *or* hear Stevie.

Carl put a small, very bright flashlight in his mouth and focused on the padlock. In his hand, he had a key ring. He inserted a key into the padlock.

"Oh my God," Steve said, wonder and happiness all mixed together in his voice. The glow of the flashlight was like a tiny spotlight, lighting some weird special effect as Carl pulled on the rusty hasp, then opened the door.

A wisp of dust sparkling in the light seemed to rise to heaven as the ancient door opened.

Then I saw them.

Bones. Steve's bones. There were tatters of black clothing also— the clothes Steve had worn since the first moment he'd shown himself to me.

I didn't have time to think, to feel. This was my boyfriend's body. This could make me lose him forever. But I had to capture his killer. That quest blocked every other thought.

Slowly, I inched toward Carl, capturing all this on my cell's video camera.

Carl began to methodically load the bones into the bag.

This was it: Carl would finally pay for Steve's death. As I inched closer and closer, concentrating on recording all this, my foot slipped. As I tried to keep my balance, I stumbled. Some apprentice had left a piece of rope out.

Carl's head jerked around, the flashlight still in his mouth.

The light was blinding me. I had to act fast, or Stevie and I both might be haunting this place forever.

I hadn't planned on this. I was just supposed to get it all on video. This wasn't supposed to turn physical. Carl would do something to prove he was Steve's killer, and then he would leave. After that, I could go to the police.

I had to think fast, or I might end up sleeping with the 'goyles.

"Carl?" I said, quietly.

Carl's flashlight still blinded me. I pushed forward.

"A little cleanup, Carl?" I said, inching closer.

Keep calm. This might work. Just push forward, little by little.

Well, at least I knew what I was thinking. But I didn't know what Carl was thinking, and it scared the hell out of me.

I kept creeping forward. Carl just stood there, as if he was made of stone, the same stone of the gargoyles that witnessed this.

It seemed like an eternity before I was close enough to knock the flashlight from his mouth. He let out a little yelp. He sounded surprised, like he didn't expect me to do that, like that hadn't been part of his plan.

Then he finally sprang to life and slapped my cell phone from my hand.

I heard two clinks, the flashlight and the cell phone hitting the floor.

I pounced. The bag of bones fell. We struggled. He pushed me back. I stumbled but managed to stay upright. I bent over and rammed him with my head. I heard a loud *ummph* as Carl exhaled, falling backward. Now I had him.

But if I didn't get him tied up, I wouldn't have him for long. Bless that shitty, careless apprentice and his rope. I looked for it frantically. It was about six feet away from me. I lunged for it.

That was enough to give Carl time to get back up. He jumped on my back, trying to pin me down. And that was his fatal mistake.

No one, but no one, stayed on my back long enough to tell the tale. I was the best in my wrestling class at that move.

In a flash, I had Carl down and had him hog-tied. That Cub Scout knot-tying badge had finally come in handy too.

He was ready for 911. I looked around for my cell phone. It had been kicked into the wall. It was pretty banged up, but it still worked. I punched in the three numbers and spilled my story to the operator.

As we waited for the cops, dead silence engulfed the cold theater. My mind, however, was shouting at me: *What a dipshit you are, Nick. What made you think Carl wouldn't fight back if he was cornered? Did you really think you could just record the whole thing, then smile and walk away? What a total fool.*

"Look at him. The kid's making a play for Artie. Do you see that, 'goyles?"

My mind was so full of my own self-loathing monologue that it took me a moment to realize that Carl was talking. But who was he talking to?

"I ought to go right up there and rip them apart. But 'goyles, Artie would leave me. He threatened to on our way here tonight."

Dionysius. This was weird. Carl was reliving that last night at the Palace, and he was telling it all to the gargoyles. The guy was totally whacked out.

"He was smiling and laughing with the guy at the burger joint drive-up window like I wasn't sitting right there next to him in the car. Well, I let him have it for that. You know what he said, 'goyles? 'Carl, you're smothering me.' Smothering him? After all I've done for him, he says that? He told me that he needed some space. Oh, I blew up over that little plan, but then he said, 'Look, Carl, either give me some space or pack your bags.' So, what can I do? I can't go over there right now."

Carl was a delusional sociopath. That much was becoming clearer and clearer, the more he talked.

"Look at 'em, 'goyles," he continued. "That kid is hugging my Artie. And that's not a 'see you later' hug like people do. No, that's a 'hold on for dear life, I love you' type hug. And I'm just supposed to stand here and take that? Uh-uh. No way. I've gotta do something, 'goyles."

"So you got even, huh, Carl?" He might be so far gone that he wouldn't answer, I thought, but I had to try.

At the sound of my voice, his head quivered or shivered or whatever. I don't know, it was like he was startled out of the *yesterday* he was reliving.

"Wha...?" he said.

"You killed Steve, didn't you, Carl?" I pressed.

"Yeah." He chuckled. It was a laugh like none I had ever heard before. Every evil in the world seemed balled up in that little laugh. "Yeah, I killed the kid. Artie'd left. Said he had a paper due, but I knew he didn't. I told him I saw through that excuse, but Artie didn't say anything. He just left. He said he'd take the bus home. Well, I knew he was all shook up from that hug, or else he woulda taken the car. Artie always took a bus ride when he wanted to *clear his head*, as he called it. I was pissed, pissed at Artie, and pissed at that little shit. I wasn't going to lose Artie to some high school kid with a stripper for a mother. I needed Artie. And, besides, Artie was better than that. So, I ran the kid over. Quick and easy. Then I dragged him back in here and got rid of him.

"I did it for Artie."

That last statement was triumphant, like it was a summing-up of his whole life, a life spent bound to Arthur Baker.

I looked around for Steve. This was the confession we had been waiting for.

But Steve wasn't there anymore.

CHAPTER 23

FOR A murder that nobody knew or cared about for over twenty years, Carl's arrest made big, big headlines for a few days. After the confession, it was like he was totally defeated, despite keeping his secret for all those years.

With the police, the reporters soon descended. I was interviewed by all the local TV stations, and my picture was plastered across the front page of the *Trib* next morning. I did some of my best lying that day. After all, I couldn't admit that I had any previous knowledge whatsoever of the murder. I certainly couldn't say, "Well, you see, my boyfriend is a ghost, and he was trapped in this theater until I could solve his murder."

No, I had to lie my pants off. I told anyone who listened that I had recently met Carl and Dr. Baker, and, finding out that they once worked at the Laughton, I took it upon myself to invite them to tour the theater for old time's sake.

I know it sounds bogus, but here's how it all went down: Carl didn't dispute my story because he was too far gone to care; Baker decided, apparently, that "no comment" was the best path to take; Streetwise didn't question my judgment, because who could buy such publicity as they were getting, having a hero in their midst? And I was shocked that I was being treated as a hero. After all, according to my story, I had just stumbled into capturing a murderer.

The lying was necessary—even in court, if it came to that, which eventually it did. After all, no one would believe me about Steve anyway.

Except for one person.... I had to see Layla and make her accept everything that I knew I had to tell her. And I had to spill my guts before she saw anything in the news. So after the police had cleared out of the Laughton, I went straight to Layla's. How she took it all is a story for another time.

As for Steve, I never saw him again. I got so caught up in first solving his murder, and then all the stuff that came after I got Carl, what I had done just washed over me. But after the cops had gone, after the reporters had cleared out, and I was alone with just the gargoyles, it began to sink in. Steve was gone.

Steve was gone, and he wasn't coming back. A gloom settled over me for a while there. I'm not going to lie to you. A gloom settled over me for quite a while. In fact, I still get a little teary when I think of him. He was my first, you know. And you never forget your first.

But what I did for Steve was right. No one should be trapped, be shackled in a prison he's not responsible for. No, letting Steve go was the only thing I could have done.

And funny thing—my cell phone video proved that Zach had it right when he created that special ghost effect for the show. And Steve had it wrong... that *is* the way it works, it seems. The minute that wisp of dust ascended into the light, Steve was gone.

I miss him so much, man, but I mean, really—could I have lived a whole lifetime with a ghost for a boyfriend? At least now I know that I helped Steve out. That means a lot to me.

I read that some artist once said that everyone would have fifteen minutes of fame in his life, and I had mine around school for the next few days, but, like most hero stories, I was soon forgotten. The head cheerleader got pregnant by the biology teacher (of all people), and my little murder-solving trick was no longer the main topic of high school gossip.

I kept reading the *Trib* every day, long after the story was pushed to the back pages. About a month after the arrest, I saw a tiny story: "Crevette Theater Hires New Second in Command." I read that one Marian Russell had been hired to replace Dr. Arthur Baker, who had recently resigned his post. The story went on to praise Dr. Russell's credentials and to recount Baker's relationship to the accused murderer Carl Kinman.

Reading that story reminded me (as if the task had ever left my mind over the last month) that I needed to face the music with Dr. Nichols. Thanks to me, he had lost his most trusted professor. He hadn't contacted me—no doubt because he had been busy finding Baker's replacement—but I was certain that he'd want to rescind the scholarship offer.

I punched in his number, and surprisingly, he answered personally.

"Nichols here."

"Dr. Nichols, this is Nick Fortunati."

"Nick.... I've been meaning to call you, but things have been absolutely insane around here. You most likely know about our big staff change, but even my secretary seems to have deserted me... for a while at least—she's on family leave."

"I wanted to call to tell you how sorry I am about the Dr. Baker thing."

"Thank you, Nick. Arthur has been a good friend for many years."

This was not going to be easy, I thought.

"Dr. Nichols, about the scholarship...."

"Yes? I briefed Dr. Russell on you, and she is really excited. That's why I've been trying to get time to call you. She wants to meet with you."

I was in shock.

"But what about Dr. Baker's leaving? That doesn't affect the scholarship?"

"Not at all... oh, we did suffer a tad bit of bad publicity here, but we can weather that storm."

"But because of me, Dr. Baker was exposed as a drug dealer. Even though that was a long time ago and he had nothing to do with Steve Stripling's murder, if I hadn't exposed Carl, you'd still have your friend working for you."

"Look, Nick, Arthur's leaving was a great loss, to our department and to me personally. As I said before, Arthur is my friend. If he's made some bad choices over the years, it is not for me to judge.

"All this publicity has been unfortunate. It no doubt has done irreparable damage to Arthur's reputation. And there is another aspect to it that I am not at liberty to discuss, although, as Arthur has admitted, secrets have a way of getting out.

"Suffice it to say that none of this has anything to do with you and your future here at U Theater. We are still extremely pleased that you will be joining us in the fall. And, that being said, when can you meet with Dr. Russell?"

I made the appointment and rang off. Dr. Nichols had been cryptic about Dr. Baker, but, just as he predicted, secrets were revealed during Carl's murder trial and its outcome. It seems that even though Dr. Baker hadn't dealt any drugs in years, he had been a user during his entire career. Some people just seem to be able to function no matter what shit they put into their systems, apparently. But Dr. Baker must have revealed this secret to Dr. Nichols, and that had to have been, ultimately, what led to his leaving Crevette.

But all that came out months after my phone call to Dr. Nichols. After I rang off that day, my first reaction was to make a beeline to the Laughton to tell Steve the good news.

My heart soon fell, realizing that Steve was just a memory now.

Then my anxiety level rose again. I had the scholarship—not just a maybe, but a solid, honest to God, full ride theater scholarship.

So it was time to face—you guessed it—my dad. And this was something I couldn't do on the phone. I grabbed a latte for courage, and then I headed to Dad's office.

"Well, well, well…," Dad greeted me as I came into his lab. "My son the hero, everybody," he said loudly so that everyone could hear.

Heads turned from lab tables, and then the techies applauded. I felt heat rising in my cheeks as I blushed.

After the applause died down and the heads turned back around, Dad pulled me into an office and motioned for me to sit.

"You know, Nick, they're announcing the scholarship next week. And I hear that you are on the fast track, thanks to all that coverage in the news. Great grades aren't the only criteria for a scholarship, you know."

Suddenly I couldn't breathe. I gulped air, hoping to fill my lungs. But all I could manage were shallow breaths.

"Spill it, Nick," Dad said. "I know something's on your mind when you breathe like this. You've been like that since you were just a little thing."

I gulped air, then blurted out, "Dad, I can't take the engineering scholarship, even if they offer it." There, I'd said it. And it felt good.

I saw Dad's face darken.

He leaned in really close and whispered. I felt his hot breath in my face. "Nick, we've been over and over this. You are not throwing away your education. It just isn't going to happen." And then, for emphasis, he added, "No way."

I don't think I'd ever seen Dad quite so angry. His look scared me. I had to temper things. And quickly. Steve had said to just tell him. And now I had to.

"No—Dad." I put up my hands in a *stop* sign, hoping to calm him down. "I'm not throwing away my education. In fact, I plan to have a very good one." I breathed again, and for the first time since I arrived at Dad's, I had a long, easy breath. "Dad, I applied for a theater scholarship at Crevette, and they gave it to me. What's more—it's even better than the one your company's giving. This one is a total free ride... tuition, books, housing, and spending money."

Dad sat. He was silent for a few moments. I couldn't tell what he was thinking. If he still insisted on the engineering thing, I guessed I could just move out. After all, I had everything covered, and I would be eighteen by then.

"Nick," he finally said, standing, "I'm very, very proud of you, son. You didn't like what your old man was pushing on you, so you went out and made your own thing happen. That takes guts, boy. A full ride, you say? Fantastic!"

I was in total shock, dumbstruck. Dionysius.

Then he turned, picked up a phone, and punched in some numbers.

"Sophia." That was my mom. "Dress up real pretty tonight because we have a celebration to go to. Our son has a big surprise for you."

Mom must have asked what the surprise was because Dad said next, "Nick will tell you the news later. For now, you just concentrate on getting even more beautiful than you usually are."

Then Dad did something he hadn't done in years. He pulled me into a huge, life-squeezing bear hug.

Would that bear hug have been so forthcoming if I had come totally clean to Dad? I don't know.

I was a royal chickenshit. Dad still didn't know about the gay thing. *Maybe I'll tell him tonight during the big celebration*, I thought.

I know—you're thinking I didn't tell him. Well, you've probably never had something so monumental in your life that you needed to do. So you don't know how you'd handle it.

I'd already burst out of the engineering career closet. The other closet door would remain closed a while longer.

Small steps, you know. Small steps.

CHAPTER 24

MY BIGGEST regret is that I never got Layla to the theater to see Steve again. She would have liked that. And I know Steve would have. But how do you tell an old woman that she has a date with a ghost? And how do you convince a ghost that he needs to renew an old relationship before it's too late? Too much for me to handle, man. Too much.

At least it was while Steve was still here.

Like I told you before, after it all went down, I had to see Layla. Alone in the Laughton with just the gargoyles and no Steve, I thought of Layla. I knew I had to see her right then. She was the closest I could get to Steve, and I needed to somehow let him know about everything. I guess I thought talking to Layla would give me some of that closure I hear about on TV.

I did need closure. Not just with the Steve thing. I needed absolution for all those lies I'd told Layla. Those were weighing heavily on me.

I had called ahead, so the guy at the gate was waiting and waved me through. And, just like the first time, there was Layla, lovely as ever, on the front steps.

"Nicky, this is about the most wonderful surprise I've had in a long time. You are a sight for sore eyes, sweetie."

Layla grabbed me and hugged me. She was a loving soul. She wrapped you in her love. Made you feel warm. Made you feel safe. "Come on inside and we can catch up."

She led me to the parlor where Billy the butler had already set a tray of goodies.

"As soon as you called, I sent Billy out for some of those little white chocolate cakes you like, sugar bear," she said, motioning for me to sit.

She poured tea and placed a cake on a plate for me. When she reached for the sugar, I started to speak.

She held up her hand. "Three lumps," she said, "Ol' Layla's memory idn't gone yet."

She handed me the tea and cake.

"Now, my little love, what brings you over here in such a hurry? I know you didn't just have a sudden urge to visit an ol' pruneface like me."

I smiled. Layla was nothing if not perceptive. Not about her being a pruneface. That would never be. No, she was too perceptive not to know I was there for a reason. A giant, hard-to-tell reason.

I took a long, calming breath.

"I know you don't read the newspapers, but just in case you catch something on TV, I wanted you to hear it from me." I took a sip of tea to clear my mind.

"What?" She looked worried. "Is something wrong? Don't bother me so, Nicky."

"Well, Carl—you remember Artie Baker's friend—was arrested today."

"I knew it. That li'l pissant was going to get in trouble someday. What did he do?"

I put the teacup to my lips, and this time I took a huge gulp. Anything to delay this.

"He murdered someone."

"Murder? My Lord, I never would have thought *that* of him. Who in the wide world did he kill?"

Delaying, this time I took a bite of cake. "Mm, mm... this is so good, Layla. I love these little things."

She swatted me on the hand.

"Nicky, you're not telling me something. I can see it in your eyes. Now, come clean. Whatever it is, Layla can take it."

I looked at her for a long time, wishing I didn't have to break this news.

Finally, I had to say something. "Carl killed Steve." Three simple words that could break an old woman's heart.

"No." She jumped up and went to a window, her back to me. "That can't be. Stevie ran away. He's been gone for years. Carl was no good, but he couldn't have done something so horrible to my baby."

"It's true, Layla. He did it that last night. The closing night at the Palace." I started to rush across the room to comfort her. But maybe she needed to be alone over there, to deflect my blows.

I told her about the afternoon's string of events, omitting, of course, everything about the ghost thing.

Layla still stood with her back to me, taking it all in. As the story unfolded, she seemed to collapse in on herself. She began to sob.

I wanted to let her deal with the news on her own terms, but she looked so helpless. I couldn't take it. I got up and went to her. Placing my hands on her shoulders, I led her back to the sofa and sat her down.

"Drink this," I said, holding my tea to her lips. "It will help."

She took a sip, but she didn't take the cup. While I put the cup down, she started bawling again.

"Why, Nicky? Why would that evil man slaughter my little lamb?"

"Carl thought Steve was interested in Artie, and Carl wasn't about to lose his lover to Steve."

"Artie and Stevie? No way. Stevie was head over heels for that rich boy he had the fight with that night."

"You're right." I sat back on the sofa. "I talked to George Mervyn, and he confirmed that. Carl saw something between Artie and Steve and blew it all out of proportion, apparently."

"I hope he fries for this, Nicky. If anybody deserves the death penalty, it's that Carl. Hurting my baby like that." And again she collapsed in sobs, this time into my arms.

"It's okay, Layla. I know how you feel about Steve. I loved him too."

As soon as I said it, I knew I had blown it.

She pulled away from me and looked me in the eye. "What does that mean? And why would you be talkin' to George Mervyn?"

I was trapped. It was confession time. I couldn't lie to Layla anymore.

"You're not going to believe this, Layla, but I swear to God it's the truth."

"I know you wouldn't fib to Layla, Nicky. Now spill it."

"Well, you know how I told you I work with the Streetwise Players?"

"At the old Palace. Of course. That's what brought you to me in the first place. Your school report."

I smiled... a guilty smile because I had lied to her from the very beginning. Now I had to make it right. Spill it all. No matter how crazy or illogical the story was. Layla would hear it all. She could believe me. Or throw me out of her house.

"Layla, there was no school report. Steve wanted me to find out how he died."

"Lordy, lordy, Nicky." She caressed my cheek. "You're not makin' any sense. Let me open a window. Fresh air will clear your head a little." She started to rise, but I pulled her back down.

It was time for the full, unexpurgated story. I'd kept it from her long enough.

"I was hanging lights one Saturday...." And the whole tale tumbled from my lips.

When I finished, we just sat. I couldn't tell how she was taking it. After all, a ghost story is not something your average person can accept.

After several minutes, Layla spoke. "So Stevie found true love after all."

That's all she said. But in those words, I knew that she believed every word I had told her.

Quietly, I said, "Yes, he did."

She clasped my hands in hers.

"Thank you, Nicky."

CHAPTER 25

MOM WAS totally gorgeous the night of the celebration. Dad couldn't keep a secret if his life depended on it. He wound up telling Mom all about the scholarship, and she was so excited for me. What's more, she immediately got an appointment to get all dolled up for the big party. A party of three, but having my mom look so gorgeous and happy—just for me—and having my dad be so proud of me: that was a big, big party.

Dad was beaming. He took us to the Crystal Palm. The dinner must have cost him a fortune, but he didn't even blink when the waiter brought the check. Could things have gone any better?

I know—I know—I know. I *had* to tell him. But, like I said, small steps, small steps.

We got home about 8:30, and I was too keyed up to just stick around and drift off to dreamland. No, I needed to get out.

So I headed to Koffee Kart for a latte.

Alone with my drink—is there such a thing as a coffeeholic? I showed all the signs of a true addict… a constant need for a fix, drinking in solitary, denial. Thank God it was just coffee.

I booted up my laptop.

As everything loaded, I sipped my coffee and thought of Steve. It had been happening a lot since that last day at the theater. I would start to tear up, missing him, then I would suddenly think *hey—it's okay; you helped him find peace, and that's what's important.* And then, of course, there would be the inevitable doubts about ever finding anyone else in my life.

I surfed the web for a while as I drank. Then I landed on my favorite site. You remember, the Gay Youth Alliance thing? Suddenly, it was like I was seeing it for the first time, and there was a popup: "Join us for a meet and greet tonight from 7 to 10… free coffee and cookies."

I gulped the last of my latte, filled with resolve. *Dionysius, give me strength.* I might not have the courage yet to come out to Dad; someday, I would.

But this I could do. I was sure of it.

I stowed the laptop in my backpack, and ran to the car. The clock on the dash told me it was 9:15 already. If I hurried, I could make the last thirty minutes. I just hoped that everyone hadn't already gone home.

If anyone else had been with me in my car, they would have heard my heart thump. I was ready, but this was a monumental step. If I hadn't been racing the clock, I might have chickened out.

It was a short drive, but along the way, I reflected on everything that had gone down. And the thing that kept popping through was that I had been doing things out of my comfort zone now for a long time. The lies, the seeking out of the people in Steve's story. They were all strangers to me, and I was a loner, remember? And the biggest leap out of my comfort zone—deciding that releasing Steve was more important than my own happiness. Yeah, I had been living outside of my box, and I could stay outside for this.

I knew the way by heart, and my car almost navigated itself there. Thank Dionysius, because my mind wasn't on my driving.

I pulled in to the parking lot. The place was still brightly lit, and through the front window, I could see several people milling about.

I switched off the ignition and leapt out of the car. *You've got momentum. Don't stop. You'll lose it.*

But I knew I wouldn't.

I took the sidewalk to the front door in about three steps. Then I flung open the door and stepped inside.

My heart was pounding even louder than before. *Everyone in this room will turn around and look for that sound,* I thought.

No one noticed me. They were all busy, talking, playing pool, and just all-around having a great time. I cautiously took a few steps into the room.

Then, from out of the crowd, a familiar face appeared. He walked across the room and took my hand.

"Nice frames." I loved that smile. "Who helped you pick those out?"

RUSSELL J. SANDERS is a lifelong devotee of the theater. He's a singer, actor, and director, winning awards for his acting roles and shows he has directed. As a teacher, he has taught theater arts to hundreds of students, plus he's also taught literature and writing to thousands of others.

Russell has also travelled the world, visiting Indonesia, Japan, India, Canada, the Caribbean, London, Amsterdam, Paris, Rome, Florence, and Venice—and almost all the US states. His friends think he's crazy, but wherever he goes, he seeks out Mexican restaurants. The Mexican food in Tokyo was great, he says; in Rome, not so good. Texans cut their teeth on barbecue and Mexican food. Russell's love for enchiladas led him on a quest to try them wherever he can find them, and he has found them in some very out-of-the-way places. And good or bad, he's delighted to sample his favorite food.

Most importantly, Russell is an out-and-proud gay man, living in Houston with his life partner of almost twenty years. He hopes that his novels inspire confidence and instill pride in his young gay fans, and he hopes others learn from his work, as well.

Find him on the web at http://russelljsanders.weebly.com

and on Facebook at https://www.facebook.com/russell.sanders.14.

Also from HARMONY INK PRESS

GHOST SONGS

ANDREW DEMCAK

http://www.harmonyinkpress.com

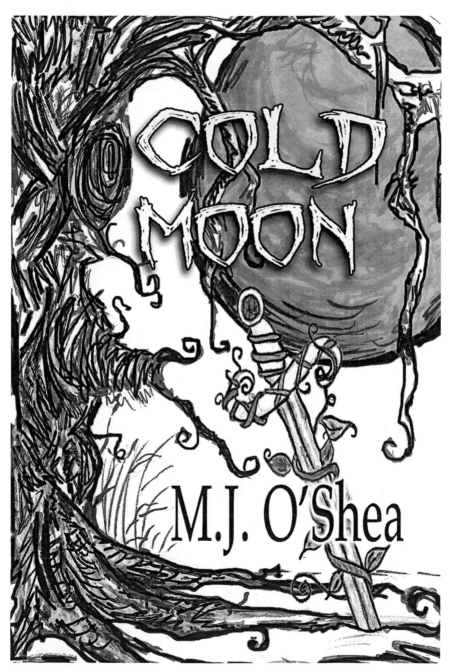

Also from HARMONY INK PRESS

EVOLUTION
SAM KADENCE

http://www.harmonyinkpress.com

Harmony Ink

CPSIA information can be obtained at www.ICGtesting.com
Printed in the USA
BVOW03s0259040614

355172BV00032B/410/P